7KP-11

P9-ARK-278

Hopkinsville-Christian County Public Library
1101 BETHEL STREET
HOPKINSVILLE, KENTUCKY 42240

GAYLORD RG

FEB 2010

OUTLAW
CANYON

**Center Point
Large Print**

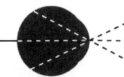

**This Large Print Book carries the
Seal of Approval of N.A.V.H.**

OUTLAW CANYON

LEWIS B. PATTEN

CENTER POINT PUBLISHING
THORNDIKE, MAINE

This Center Point Large Print edition
is published in the year 2010 by arrangement with
Golden West Literary Agency.

Copyright © 1961 by Lewis B. Patten.
Copyright © renewed 1989 by Catherine C. Patten.

All rights reserved.

The text of this Large Print edition is unabridged.
In other aspects, this book may vary
from the original edition.
Printed in the United States of America
on permanent paper.
Set in 16-point Times New Roman type.

ISBN: 978-1-60285-651-6

Library of Congress Cataloging-in-Publication Data

Patten, Lewis B.
   Outlaw canyon / Lewis B. Patten.
      p. cm.
   ISBN 978-1-60285-651-6 (library binding : alk. paper)
   1. Large type books. I. Title.

PS3566.A79O87 2010
813'.54--dc22

2009033914

CHAPTER 1

The wind came up at nightfall, whispering softly at first out of the southwest. It sighed down off the precipitous rims of Fortress Mesa, whose nearly flat top towered fifteen hundred feet above the equally flat bench on which sprawled the log house and outbuildings of Fortress Ranch. It increased rapidly in intensity as the minutes passed, until it was whipping and tearing at the trees in the yard, banging unfastened doors and occasionally ripping a split cedar shingle from the roof of the ancient barn.

At nine the rain began, with pelting, stinging small drops that quickly increased in both size and density until it seemed as though gigantic hands were pouring the torrent with careless cruelty upon the land.

Inside the huge living room of the thick-walled ranch house, Chris Knudson sat staring moodily into the crackling fire in the fireplace. His eyes were faded blue, the skin of his face brown and shiny and brittle with age and illness. The backs of his hands, resting upon his bony knees, were blue-veined and frail for all their size. His body, as heavy-boned as his hands, was gaunt almost to emaciation. His clothes hung loosely, reminders that when they were new his body had been healthy and muscular and strong.

Strange and compelling emotions were within this man of late. Emotions unfamiliar to him. Defeat. Puzzlement and confusion. Regret and sometimes a vaguely unformed wish that he could go back and change the things he had so obviously done wrong.

But it was too late now. The expression in his faded eyes said he knew that too. It was too late for going back. There was only time to play out his life's remaining scenes, however unpleasant and bitter they might be. And for the tragedy that must inevitably climax the final one.

He frowned heavily, the confusion strong in him. He had not sown hate, so why should he reap it now? He had been a fool, perhaps, and too busily engrossed in the everlasting fight to build and hold this ranch.

But he had given generously to Wes of material things. The boy had owned a pony at six, a horse of his own at nine. At fourteen he'd had a gun. He had money to spend and . . .

When had it begun? When had it really begun? Early, Chris supposed, and perhaps Mary had been right in trying to protect Wes from the dangers inherent in the operation of a ranch. Perhaps Chris had been wrong in trying to make Wes do the things other boys did—chores when he was small, riding and other work when he was old enough.

He got up, stalked to the fireplace and turned his

back to it, shivering. He could hear the unrestrained fury of the storm outside, pelting against the windows, driving against the roof, cascading in torrents from the eaves. He heard the kitchen door open and felt the rush of air that came in, that pushed through the house and departed up the fireplace flue. He waited expectantly and a few moments later Matt Springer entered the room, dripping, wiping his face with a towel.

Matt was tall, six-one, whip slender and in his mid-twenties. His eyes were blue, wide-set and sharp beneath brows unexpectedly shaggy for a man his age. His jaw was long, hard, covered with a light stubble of yellow whiskers. His hair, the color of his beard, was soaked, and short, and made tiny ringlets on his head.

He came over to the fire and spread his hands to it. After a moment he reached under his soaked jacket and brought out tobacco and papers which were only slightly damp. He rolled a cigarette, lighted it and drew deeply of the smoke.

His eyes rested steadily on old Chris's face as he said, "Some storm."

Chris nodded. Why Wes couldn't have been like Matt, he wondered. Matt had become exactly what he'd wanted his own son to be. The reasons for that were obscure to him though. Matt hadn't had half the chance Wes had. He hadn't even had a home until the night Chris picked him up, dirty and half starved, in the freight yards at Denver, where he'd gone with a trainload of steers.

He shook his head confusedly. He had certainly given Matt no more than he had his son. Or had he?

He asked, "What was the difference between you and him, Matt? Why should he hate me the way he does? He'd have to hate me to do the things he's done."

It was a moment before Matt answered him. "He's got to blame somebody besides himself and you're handiest, I guess. He hates me too."

"But what went wrong? For God's sake, what went wrong, and when?"

Matt frowned. He drew deeply on his cigarette and stared thoughtfully into the flames. "I've thought about that and wondered about it. Your missus started things, I guess, by being afraid Wes was going to get hurt. You'd tell him to do something and she'd tell him he didn't have to." He smiled faintly. "Not your fault that it made you mad. Not so unusual that it made you tougher on Wes than you might otherwise have been. But pretty soon he was thinking of her as the one who stuck up for him and of you as the one who picked on him."

"But later—my God, I fished him out of every damned jam he ever got into. Why?"

"Too late then, I guess." Matt stopped and stared at the old man with sympathy in his eyes. "Stop beating yourself over the head, Chris. You didn't plant the hate in him. It happened, that's all."

Chris turned around and stared into the flames. Such little things seemed to guide the destinies of men. Why had Matt turned out so different from Wes?

He'd made Matt work from the time he'd brought him home. He'd put him to doing chores at first. Later he'd put him to building fence. When he was big enough, he'd let him ride with the crew. He had certainly given Matt no love. For a long time he'd felt nothing at all for him.

Matt himself had earned his respect. By being what he was. By accepting responsibility in his tough, determined way. But then Chris hadn't had Mary working against him with regard to Matt.

He didn't blame her even now. She was gone and his memories of her were mostly sweet. She just hadn't belonged out here. This wild and open country had been a fearsome thing to her until the day she died. She had tried to protect Wes after he began to grow, never realizing perhaps that he was not an infant anymore. She had thought Chris harsh because he expected so much of the boy.

He shrugged fatalistically. Thinking of the past and of the mistakes he had made was a dreary business that only served to further discourage him. He said, "What are we going to do now?"

Matt met his glance steadily. "They've driven five hundred head of Fortress cattle into Outlaw

Canyon and we don't dare let it go. The only thing to do is swear out warrants for Olguin, the Taskers and Wes. We get the sheriff and a posse and ride in there. There's no other way."

"What if he . . . ?" Chris's voice was almost a whisper.

Matt didn't reply to the half-uttered question. There was no answer he could make, Chris realized. Matt certainly couldn't assure him that his son would not be killed. Nobody could do that. At last Matt said reluctantly, "You've got no other choice. Taking a herd that size was a deliberate slap in the face, a dare. If you don't take it up and go after them, they'll come after us. They won't stand still; it's gone too far for that. They're not after the five hundred cattle they stole from you anyway. They're after your hide."

Chris nodded reluctantly. "I guess you're right." In spite of the heat from the fireplace, he felt cold.

Matt said, "I'll ride to town first thing in the morning and swear out warrants in your name."

Chris nodded. "All right, Matt: If you think it's the only way."

Matt met his glance unflinchingly. "That's what I think but it's still up to you. If you say no, we'll try and work it out some other way."

For a moment there was something of the old toughness in the way Chris looked at him. He said, "You see Sherm Logan tomorrow."

He stood in front of the fire a moment more.

Then he said, "Guess I'll go on up to bed. Good night, Matt."

"Good night, Chris."

Chris walked unsteadily across the room to the stairs. He climbed them heavily. For several moments his tread was audible to Matt. Then a door closed and all was still.

Matt turned and stared into the leaping flames. The rain hammered mercilessly against the house, driven by the fury of the wind. The legs of his pants began to steam.

He made another cigarette and smoked it, frowning thoughtfully.

He had been fourteen when Chris picked him up. Fourteen and homeless and dirty and hungry. He had never liked remembering the things that had happened at home to make him run away but it didn't hurt so much now.

He'd been raised on a Kansas farm. Not a good farm. Just a barren place with the original sod shanty sitting in the middle of it. There was never enough to eat and in winter never enough clothes to keep him warm.

His father had a job in town at the livery barn. And often as not, on payday, he stayed in town. He stayed at the saloon until he couldn't even walk. Then, next day, he'd come dragging home. Sick and ashamed and bringing all the food he had been able to buy with the little money he had left.

On one such night an early blizzard struck,

catching Matt and his mother without enough fuel to keep the shanty warm. To make things worse, a window blew out and by the time they got it boarded up, both were chilled to the bone.

Nervously Matt rolled another cigarette. His face was pale, his mouth tight with the memory of that night. Come morning, his mother was dead. And he was nearly so.

He left and managed to walk to town. He warmed himself by a fire a hobo had built beside the railroad tracks at the edge of town. When the train came through, he caught it and rode west with the hobo, not even caring which direction he went or where he stopped.

Denver happened to be the place because the two were routed from their car by a railroad detective. Broke, half starved, he was picked up by Chris Knudson and fed. When Chris offered him a home he accepted because there was nothing else he could do.

There had been a long time, he remembered, when he promised himself he would one day return to the homestead in Kansas and kill his father for what he had done. But as he grew older, the need for vengeance died. Now he had no intention of ever going back. Sometimes he could even feel a certain compassion for his father and for the weakness that had made him unable to face poverty without the crutch of liquor that made it bearable.

Those first months at Fortress Ranch had not

been easy ones. He'd been thin and undernourished and he wasn't very strong. The work he was given to do tired him before the day had scarcely begun. But he stuck to it doggedly, afraid Chris Knudson would kick him out.

Why Wes, Chris's son, had formed such a dislike toward him, he'd never known. It couldn't have been jealousy because Matt had possessed nothing he could be jealous of.

But the animosity had been there from the first. It showed itself in little cruelties that Matt hadn't dared resent. Outwardly at least.

Inwardly he resented them deeply, more so because he was jealous of all the things Wes had. His face felt hot now as he remembered that jealousy and what it had made him do.

Wes taunted him continuously. Matt avoided fighting with him until one day Wes taunted him in Chris's presence and Chris said, "I'd bust him for that if I was you."

Matt took him at his word. He busted Wes in the mouth and followed through so savagely that after two or three minutes Chris pulled him off.

Now he realized that jealousy and not resentment of the taunts had prompted his savagery. Afterward he'd expected Chris to tell him to leave, but Chris hadn't said a word.

Things had been different between Chris and his son after that, though. Wes resented the fact that Chris had urged Matt to start the fight. He'd been ashamed because he hadn't shown up well. And he'd blamed Matt for it.

That had been ten years ago. Matt left the fire and walked to the window. He stared at the rain streaming down the window panes. Ten years ago, yet perhaps it had been the beginning of this. Perhaps it had started Wes along the road he now traveled, although plenty of other things had happened since. Scowling, Matt returned to the fire and glared down into it. He heard a sound upstairs and listened intently. Then he relaxed again.

Maybe, he thought, there was still time for Chris to patch things up with Wes. If he himself packed up and left.

But he knew that was only wishful thinking. Things had gone too far. Even if Wes had been of a mind to patch things up and change, which Matt doubted, it was too late. He was solidly aligned with the Taskers and Rudy Olguin. He spent all of his time with them, mostly inside Outlaw Canyon, the virtually impregnable home of the Tasker clan which had been a haven for outlaws as long as Matt could recall.

Twenty miles long and a fourth that wide, its only entrance was through a narrow gorge which a handful of men could successfully defend against an army. Matt had never been inside the canyon proper, only in the gorge itself, so he really didn't know what he'd be running into tomorrow. He might never see the inside of it.

He might be killed before he got that far.

But he had to try. Outlaw Canyon had to be cleaned out. The brazen theft of five hundred Fortress cattle proved it now if nothing had before.

Matt suspected that there was a lot more to the theft of the big herd than was immediately apparent. First, Fortress's crew and Matt himself had been drawn away from the home range by a drifter's false report of having seen Fortress beef being driven off the far side of Fortress Mesa. But when they returned, they'd have had to be blind to miss the plain tracks the Taskers had left everywhere as they openly gathered up a herd and drove it into the canyon.

It looked as if they had baited a trap and Matt knew he might be making a mistake in taking the bait. But he wasn't a man for playing devious games with anyone. He figured he and the crew, the sheriff and a posse, would be enough men to force a way even into Outlaw Canyon. Sherm Logan would be reluctant but under the circumstances he could hardly refuse to lend his authority and status to what Fortress meant to do.

Matt had a strong suspicion that the Taskers' carefully baited trap might be meant to eliminate him and thus demoralize the Fortress crew. He shrugged. That was a chance he'd have to take. A lot of people were going to get hurt before this thing was over. But there was no other way that Matt could see.

CHAPTER 2

The fury of the storm continued unabated. Matt Springer, his clothes dry from the fire's heat, moved away from it, went to the window and stared moodily outside.

What of Josie Tasker? What would happen to her when Fortress rode, with the sheriff and his posse, into Outlaw Canyon to serve the warrants?

He left the window and angrily began to pace back and forth from one end of the room to the other. He supposed Josie and he had been partly responsible, at least, for the present tension between the Taskers and Fortress Ranch. He frowned, remembering.

The year following Matt's arrival at Fortress, Chris Knudson had decided he ought to go to school. And so he'd ridden, every day, to the little one-room log schoolhouse at the mouth of Outlaw Canyon, nine miles from the ranch.

Wes went there too, but the two never rode together. And that first year had not been easy for Matt.

Fifteen, he was. He could read a little. His mother had taught him that. But he had never gone to school. He was at least six years behind the other kids his age.

They laughed at him and taunted him. But stubbornly he continued to recite when called upon though his face burned and his whole body felt hot.

He would read stumblingly from a book, or would falter through an arithmetic problem that the others his age could do with ease. His discomfort and embarrassment only made him more determined to learn and to catch up. And Josie Tasker had a part in that.

At fourteen, she was a thin and leggy girl. Her face was intense, brown, dominated by eyes that seemed too large for it. She wore her flaming hair in pigtails, each tied with a bit of ribbon at its end.

Greenish eyes. A bridge of freckles across her nose. And that flaming hair, that had darkened as she grew older to a deep shade of copper red.

He found her sitting her horse squarely in the trail one afternoon in late October as he rode toward home. He stopped, and stared at her suspiciously, suspecting some new prank on the part of those who had been tormenting him. He stared around warily at the golden underbrush.

Josie flushed but her eyes didn't waver from his face. She said, "There's no one else. I'm all alone."

"What do you want?"

Her flush deepened but still she didn't look away. "Haven't you ever been to school before?"

Matt shook his head dumbly.

"You don't know much, do you?"

"I'll learn." His anger was rising. He touched his

horse's sides with his heels and started to go on past.

She said, "I could maybe help you a little bit."

He stared at her suspiciously.

"I mean it. I'm not teasing. We could go back to the school and I could help you until it's dark."

"Why?"

Now her eyes fell away from his. "I don't know. Maybe it just makes me mad to see them all teasing you the way they do. I'll bet you could just show 'em if you wanted to."

"Maybe. Maybe not."

"You want me to help you some?"

"I guess so." He was still suspicious but for the first time hope was stirring in him. Maybe he *could* catch up. It wouldn't hurt anything to try.

"Come on then." She rode past him and headed back toward the school.

He stared closely and suspiciously at her face as she went past. He wondered if this was some new trick, if the others wouldn't be waiting when they reached the school. He hesitated, on the point of riding away toward home. Then, suddenly he followed her. If it was a trick, if they were waiting for him with some new prank, it wasn't going to hurt him any more than the others had.

She rode without looking back until they reached the school. It was deserted. The teacher's buggy was gone and so were the horses of the other kids. He slid off and tied his horse. So did Josie.

She went inside and he followed her. She got her books from her desk and sat down. Matt sat down at the desk next to her.

That afternoon, both of them fumbled helplessly with what they were trying to do. Josie knew nothing at all about teaching. But she tried to do as Miss Foster did, and it was a surprise to them both when it became too dark to see.

Leaving, Josie said, "We'll do the same thing tomorrow and every day. You just ride away like you were going home and then come back."

"All right."

They stood there staring at each other for a minute more. Then both silently mounted and rode away toward home.

That day was sharp and clear in Matt's memory. All of the ones that followed it were not. But he had progressed. He had learned to read with surprising speed, and to spell, and to work out simple problems in arithmetic. The taunting, which had so embarrassed him, gradually stopped.

It was spring before Wes Knudson noticed that Matt was always a couple of hours late arriving home from school. Matt never knew what made him notice at all. But when he did, he trailed him back. Then he rode up into Outlaw Canyon and told Wiley Tasker, one of Josie's brothers, that she and Matt were carrying on at the school after the other kids were gone.

Wiley didn't wait to confront Josie with his accusation. He galloped down to the school that same afternoon.

He missed catching them at the schoolhouse. He missed seeing Josie at all. But he got ahead of Matt and caught him as he came up the steep trail to the bench about six-thirty that night.

Matt had grown like a weed that winter. He was almost six feet tall, though he had not yet begun to fill out and was stringy and thin as a bean.

He was startled when he saw Wiley Tasker in the trail ahead of him. Wiley said, "You son of a bitch, I'll learn you to mess with Josie like you been doin' all winter."

Matt said, "I ain't—she—"

Wiley raked his horse and plunged toward him. Wiley's hands went out and yanked Matt from his saddle. Matt thumped on the ground and the fall knocked the breath out of him. Gasping, he got halfway to his feet, protesting, "I—we—"

He didn't get a chance to finish. Wiley's fist smashed his mouth and drove him back to the ground again.

He got up, dodging as Tasker swung at him. He circled warily, trying desperately to get his breath.

It was almost dark. But the sky still held some of dusk's deep gray, shedding a small amount of light upon the two. Matt gasped, "Damn it, we ain't done nothin' wrong. You ask Josie."

"Sweet-talked her 'til she'd lie, have you? God damm it, I ought to kill you right here an' now." Wiley lunged toward him, catching Matt in the belly with a wild and savage swing.

Matt bent double with the pain. Tasker caught him with a chopping left as his head came down. Matt slammed back into a high clump of brush. Tasker was on him like a wolf.

Matt raised a knee to defend himself. It caught Tasker squarely in the face. Blood spurted from his nose. He brushed it away with a sleeve, then glanced down at the bloody sleeve in surprise.

Matt rolled, trying to escape the clawing tangle of brush. Wiley Tasker came after him. Matt rolled clear, under Tasker's horse. The animal danced nervously, trying to avoid Matt's body with his hoofs. Matt got up immediately beneath the horse, bumping his head against the horse's flank.

The animal kicked viciously. The kick caught Tasker squarely in the chest as he lunged toward Matt.

He grunted monstrously and slammed back, disappearing momentarily into the shadows of the brush. Matt got up and went after him, angry enough now to try fighting, on equal terms, a man half again as heavy as he and both stronger and more experienced.

But Tasker had lost all his fight. He lay spread-eagled on the ground, not unconscious but nearly so. Matt stood over him and said, "Damn you, you just talk to Josie when you get home. We ain't done nothing wrong. She's been helping me to catch up in school, that's all."

Tasker didn't answer him. Matt walked to his horse and swung to his back. He left and rode on home.

Next day, Josie Tasker had a black eye and a split lip. Matt stared at her furtively all day, infuriated by what they had done to her because of him.

He tried to catch her when she left, but she fled like a frightened deer. He returned to the schoolhouse as usual to wait for her.

The minutes stretched into hours and at last light faded and the land grew dark. Josie didn't come. She would never come again.

And now he remembered that Wes had avoided him all day. Even when he'd come face to face with Wes at recess, Wes had refused to meet his eyes. It added up. Wes, curious because he was habitually late from school, had followed and spied on him. And Wes had told Wiley Tasker, coloring the story enough so that Wiley believed the worst.

Infuriated, Matt went looking for Wes when he got home, and caught him coming out of the kitchen door. He grabbed Wes's arm. "You're the one who told on us. Ain't you?"

"Told who about what?"

"Told Wiley Tasker that Josie an' me were studyin' late at school. Only you told him something else."

"What if I did?" Wes was scared, but defiant too. "What you goin' to do about it?"

Matt was still sore from the fight with Wiley Tasker the night before. But when he struck out, it was not so much for his own hurts as for those of Josie Tasker, who had only tried to help him, who had given generously of her time and who had only been hurt in return. The blow struck Wes in the mouth and knocked him stumbling back into the kitchen door.

Matt followed, to be stopped by Wes's mother, who held a frying pan tremblingly in both her hands. She screamed, "You savage, get out of here! Get off this ranch! I've had all I'm going to stand of you and the way you're always tormenting Wes!"

Matt backed out the door. When he was clear of it, he turned and ran—squarely into old Chris, who was coming from the barn.

"Whoa! What the hell's this all about?"

"Nothin'. I just hit Wes."

"What for?"

"You go ask Wes. I hit him, that's all. I'll get my stuff and get going. Tonight."

"Get going? What the devil are you talking about?"

"She told me to. Mrs. Knudson told me to."

"Well, I'm tellin' you to stay. Now get on out to the bunkhouse and don't give me any more of your lip."

Matt went. He didn't know what was said up at the house, but later Chris came to the bunkhouse and beckoned him out. He said, "You're staying, understand. It'll be all right." He studied Matt perplexedly for several moments. At last he said, "Josie Tasker, huh? Well I'll be damned!"

He turned and strode away into the night. Matt may have been mistaken, but he thought he heard Chris chuckling.

It was all that was ever said, then or later. The incident seemed to be closed, but Matt had the feeling it was not. He and the incident itself had been another wedge driven between Chris Knudson and his son, between Chris and his ailing wife.

Matt nervously rolled himself another cigarette. A small thing, perhaps, that incident. None of the incidents had been big.

Yet in the aggregate they had added up to something big. Something big enough to split Chris Knudson and his wife apart, big enough to make Wes Knudson hate his father as much as he hated Matt.

He scowled and kicked out angrily at a stool, then pulled the kick before it struck. He walked to the window nervously and stared at the streaming panes. Every stream in the country would be bank full tomorrow and the river would be a raging torrent tearing westward toward the sea. Bridges would be out and . . .

But the floods wouldn't stop Fortress from riding into Outlaw Canyon tomorrow. Nothing on earth could stop that now.

CHAPTER 3

Matt only went to school for a year. Wes finished the same year and went east to college. During the succeeding two years, until Wes was expelled, Mrs. Knudson grew weaker steadily. Chris brought doctors for her all the way from St. Louis, but it did no good. She had some kind of blood disease that was incurable. Chris, and Matt, and probably Mrs. Knudson herself, knew it was only a matter of time.

Nor did the letters that arrived several times a year from Wes's college help. He was continually in trouble. He stole a horse and buggy and wrecked the buggy when, at high speed, he put a wheel off the edge of the road. Chris sent a bank draft to cover the damages. Then Wes got a town girl pregnant and again Chris sent a draft. Next Wes and two others nearly killed a boy in a brutal hazing episode. Chris sent a draft as usual.

But when Wes was caught cheating on his exams, Chris's money couldn't get him out of it. He was sent home, expelled.

Wes was both sullen and arrogant when he came home. He began spending more and more of his time in town. There were gambling debts, which Chris paid for him. There were other things. Matt never knew how many times Chris bailed his son out of trouble or how many checks he wrote.

In the meantime, Matt worked steadily on the ranch. And Chris grew to depend upon him more and more. Often he said, with weary discouragement, "I wish to God Wes was like you, Matt. Why couldn't he have been interested in the ranch?"

Matt seldom answered that, unless it was to reassure Chris that eventually Wes would come home, that eventually he would exhibit interest in the ranch. Or he would say, "Wes is just sowin' wild oats, Chris. He'll be all right." But even as he said the words he knew they weren't true. Wes wasn't going to change.

Wes had been home almost a year when Mrs. Knudson died. Matt knew he would never forget that night, nor the look that had been on Chris's face as he stood over Matt's bunk holding a lamp and saying, "Matt, go to town and get Wes. Mary's dead."

Matt got up immediately. He pulled on his pants and boots and strapped on his gun. Shrugging into a shirt, he went outside to where Chris waited for him with the lamp.

Chris's face was gray and his eyes were filled with pain. Matt asked worriedly, "Is there anything I can do before I go?"

Chris shook his head. Almost dazedly he said, "She wanted Wes at the last, Matt. She wanted Wes instead of me. She blamed me because he wasn't here. Said I'd driven him away."

"She was sick, Chris. She didn't know what she was saying."

Chris shook his head numbly. "She knew. I guess I've been wrong, Matt. But I'll make it up to him. I swear I will."

"Sure you will, Chris." Helplessly Matt left him and went to the corral. He caught himself a horse, saddled and rode away toward town. Chris still stood dazedly in the middle of the yard, holding the lamp.

Matt reached town just before midnight. It was Saturday night and the saloons were still open. Here and there a lone drunk wandered along the street toward home.

He began making the rounds. He found Wes in the second saloon he visited, the Red Dog. Wes was in a poker game. His eyes were red and he hadn't shaved for a couple of days. A bottle and glass sat on the table beside him.

Matt crossed the room. He stood looking at Wes for several moments before Wes glanced up.

Wes had changed. He was thinner than he had ever been before.

Though thinner, he was as tall as Matt. Instead of the range clothes that Matt wore, he wore a townsman's suit. The grip of a double-barreled derringer protruded from his vest pocket. In addition, he wore a six shooter, in a tied-down holster hanging low at his side. Matt remembered thinking that Chris would do his son a favor when he stopped paying him out of jams, when he forced Wes to stand on his own two feet. But he didn't suppose Chris would ever do it.

Hatred blazed immediately in Wes's eyes. He asked harshly, "What the hell do *you* want?"

"Chris sent me to bring you home."

Wes mimicked savagely, "Chris sent you to bring me home! Well just go back and tell Chris I ain't comin' home. Not tonight or any other night!"

Matt's patience might have held out except for the fact that Wiley Tasker, across from Wes, chose this moment to laugh.

Thinking about it now, he admitted to himself that his actions had been colored by dislike for Wiley, by memory of the time Wiley had caught and beaten him on the way home from school, and he remembered the black eye and split lip which Josie had worn to school next day.

He swung angrily toward Tasker. His foot went out, hooked a leg of Wiley's tilted chair and yanked.

Wiley spilled backward with a high, thin yell of surprise. He grabbed the poker table as he went down and pulled it on top of him. He struggled several moments with the table and chair, rolled clear and yanked out his gun.

Matt stepped close and kicked it out of his hand. He turned his head toward Wes. "Chris said to bring you home. Your mother's—"

He didn't get a chance to finish. Wiley Tasker was up. He lunged toward Matt, colliding with him and spilling him into another table.

At this moment Wes also got into the fight. He plunged toward Matt, swinging a savage, pointed boot that caught Matt squarely in the face.

Matt went down again into the tangle of overturned table, chairs and men struggling to get to their feet and get away. On hands and knees he scrambled away, avoiding Wes's second kick, and made it to his feet. Tasker lunged at him from one direction, Wes Knudson from the other. Matt braced himself and swung.

His fist struck Tasker in the belly and doubled him. Mercilessly Matt brought up his knee, which caught Tasker in the jaw as his head came down.

He straightened from the force of it, his eyes glazed. Matt turned to meet Wes and sidestepped nimbly as he came past. Wes slammed head-on into Wiley Tasker and the pair went down in a heap.

Someone yelled. "Look out, Matt!" and he swung his head. Floyd Tasker, Wiley's brother, was coming at him from behind, swinging a chair.

He tried to duck it and failed. The chair smashed as it struck him on top of the head, but the blow was damaging, even so. It drove him to his knees, stunned.

He reached up and swiped a hand across his bleeding mouth where Wes's boot had struck. He shook his head angrily, trying to make it clear. Floyd Tasker flung aside the broken chair and came after him.

Matt tried to get up but one knee was still on the floor when Floyd's roundhouse struck. Squarely in the throat it took him and for several moments his breathing stopped with the excruciating pain of it. Doubled on the floor, he gagged and choked and fought for air. Tasker stood over him, kicking brutally. Every kick landed and every kick burned like hell as it did. Matt grunted, and gasped, but at last he succeeded in drawing air into his lungs.

His body was a flaming mass of pain. His throat was on fire and so were his straining lungs. Blood trickled from both corners of his mouth.

But suddenly there was something in him that had not been there before. Rage. Pure, undiluted fury. It brought him stumbling to his feet in spite of Floyd's swinging boots. It sent him staggering toward the man.

Not since he had been fully grown had Matt been in a fight. It surprised him now to realize he was a full two inches taller than Floyd. He was heavier too, and when his fist struck Floyd the man went stumbling back as though he had been kicked by a horse.

Matt followed him, pounding, cutting, bruising, absorbing Floyd's blows and scarcely noticing them.

He cut Floyd's face to ribbons and drove him all

the way across the saloon to the wall. Here he slammed him against the wall so hard that the impact rattled the bottles on the backbar.

His eyes dull, Floyd slid down the wall. Matt swung around, his eyes red and blazing, his mouth bleeding freely.

It surprised him that so little time had been consumed in ridding himself of Floyd. Across the room, Wiley and Wes were just getting up.

The crowd had scattered. Some had gone out the door. Some had taken refuge behind the bar. A few stood pressed against the wall.

Wiley started toward Matt, but Wes went after him and flung him roughly aside. He yanked the revolver from its holster and brought it up. He muttered hoarsely, "You sonofabitch, I should've done this a long time ago!"

Matt hauled up short, his mind racing furiously. He couldn't kill Chris's son. He couldn't repay all Chris had done for him this way. Not even if his refusal to do so cost him his life.

So he yelled, "Wes! Damn it, I've been trying to tell you something! Your mother's dead! That's why Chris wants you to come home!"

For several seconds, he did not think Wes had understood. The muzzle of his revolver didn't waver. Neither did the look of fury in his eyes diminish. Yet the gun didn't fire. And as the seconds dragged past, its muzzle slowly dropped.

His eyes dulling, Wes shoved the revolver into

its holster. He didn't look at Matt, but turned and stumbled toward the door and on outside.

Matt stared at Wiley Tasker, whose thoughts were written plainly on his face. He said coldly, "Go ahead, Wiley. There's nothing to keep me from killing *you!*"

Wiley froze, his hand less than an inch from the grip of his holstered gun. Matt backed deliberately toward the door.

Before he could reach it, he heard the rapid pound of hoofs in the street. He backed on out and turned his head.

His mouth split into a humorless grin and he winced as it hurt his smashed mouth. Wes had taken his horse.

He backed until he reached the darkness beyond the light streaming from the doors. Then he turned and ran toward the livery barn.

He got a horse from the hostler, mounted and rode out of town. He knew he hadn't handled this very well, but then Wes hadn't really given him the chance.

Nor had he strengthened his friendship with the Tasker clan. Not that it mattered. He'd never been friendly with them and he never would.

He didn't go into the house when he reached the ranch that night. He didn't want any more trouble with Wes because he knew it would hurt Chris.

Instead he went back to the bunkhouse and went back to bed. But he didn't sleep. He lay there until dawn, staring into the blackness, wondering what he could do to help Chris now when the old man needed help so much.

By the time dawn streaked the sky, he knew there was nothing he could do. This was a burden Chris would have to bear alone.

He was startled out of his memories by the vicious rattle of hailstones against the house. He stared at the window, watching them strike. They were marble size, but they sounded bigger than that, perhaps because of the velocity of the wind driving them.

The hail lasted several minutes. When it stopped the silence was as oppressive as the noise had been.

After the funeral, Chris's health began to fail. He lost weight until his clothes hung on his bony frame like sacks. His face grew gaunt. He lost interest in his personal appearance and it was many days sometimes between his shaves and changes of clothes.

He rode the steep, grassy acres of Fortress alone, brooding. He snapped angrily at Matt or at members of the crew when they tried to talk to him.

Matt got Doc Place to ride out and look at him, but warned him to explain his visit as accidental rather than intentional. There was a loud, bitter argument in the house between the two, but in the end Chris consented to let Doc examine him. Doc found nothing wrong.

Yet Chris continued to age. He continued to grow weaker and his interest in living did not revive. Nor was he successful in getting Wes to come home and stay. Wes just laughed at him.

And at last, he did the thing Matt thought he should have done many years ago. He stopped giving money to his son. He sent word to Wes that, unless he was willing to come home to the ranch and go to work, he was on his own.

But by the time he did it, it was too late for anything constructive to come out of it. Wes had gone too far to change.

He couldn't earn a living, or wouldn't. He had accustomed himself to a life requiring large sums of money regularly. Cut off by Chris, he took the next inevitable step. He began to steal.

CHAPTER 4

It was the following spring before Matt saw Wes again. He was returning from a check of the grass on top of Fortress Mesa, preparatory to driving a large bunch of cattle there from their winter range on the benches immediately surrounding the main buildings of the ranch.

A rain squall was sweeping across the top of Fortress Mesa like a giant broom as he halted at timber's edge on one of those benches a thousand feet below its table top. He frowned slightly as he studied some prints in the soft, black earth.

Five head of cattle, he judged. Probably three-year-olds and probably steers. Being driven by a single man.

He swung from his horse, knelt and studied the prints more closely than before. Judging the age of a set of tracks involved a lot of things, the amount of moisture in the ground, the character of the ground itself, whether the spot was in the shade or in the sun. His judgment was automatic when it came. The prints had been made today, probably before noon.

It was now late afternoon. Matt stood up and squinted against the haze lying in the river valley far below. He rolled a cigarette thoughtfully and touched the flame of a match to its end. He had a choice. He could return to the ranch, get his supper and a couple of men. He could be back here shortly after dark and they could take up the trail at dawn.

Only that would give the thief an extra four or five hours' start. Enough, perhaps, to let him get clear away.

On the other hand, if he stayed and followed the trail alone until dark, he could cut that lead. And perhaps tomorrow overtake the man.

There was a third alternative. He could return to the ranch after dark. With reinforcements he could return to whatever spot darkness had forced him to give up the trail. He shook his head almost imperceptibly. There was one rustler so it was unlikely he'd need any help. Besides, a given spot in that timber ahead wouldn't be easy in the dark. An hour or more of early daylight tomorrow might be wasted casting back and forth before they found the trail.

Once he had assessed his chances, he wasted no more time. Mounting, he put his horse into the trail which immediately entered the timber and began the long, steep descent toward the river valley far below.

The sun sank swiftly toward the horizon in the west and slid beneath it. Afterglow laid itself on the clouds overhead and on the remaining vestiges of the broom-like squall that had swept the mesa top. Both clouds and lightly falling rain turned gold, then pink, then at last dusk's gray.

Here where timber was heavy, light faded even more quickly than elsewhere and, half an hour after sunset, Matt was forced to stop. He swung down, unsaddled and picketed his horse in a small clearing with his rope. He returned to where he had left his saddle and untied the blanket roll from it. He had no food with him and so would go without supper tonight. Yet doing so didn't particularly bother him. He'd done it often enough before.

He spread the blankets on the ground and lay on them. He rolled himself up, reached out and pulled the saddle closer so his head could rest comfortably on it. He closed his eyes.

Every ranch the size of Fortress lost cattle to rustlers, he thought. It was inevitable. When the losses were made up of single animals used by neighboring small ranchers for food, nothing was ever said. But when they were driven away in bunches, and if nothing was done to stop it, the bunches became larger, the losses more noticeable. Rustling had bankrupted larger ranches than Fortress and it could happen here.

He drowsed, and fell asleep. Several times he was awakened by some night noise. Each time he immediately dropped off to sleep again.

He arose as the sky turned gray, caught and saddled his horse. Then squatted comfortably, smoking, waiting until the light would be strong enough to take up the trail.

As soon as it was, he mounted and set off

through the timber again. A couple of hours after sun-up, he reached the river valley and an hour later swam his horse across. On the far side, he scouted back and forth until he found the trail of the stolen cattle coming out.

Fresher now. Water carried out by the dripping cattle still was visible as dampened ground beside the trail. The rustler had spent the night on the far side of the river, he guessed, having held the cattle between himself and the river throughout the night. Which meant that he was now hardly more than two or three hours ahead.

Sagebrush was heavy here and as tall as a horseman's head. But the ground was soft and nearly bare of grass and it was easy to trail. Matt lifted his horse to a steady lope.

The sun crawled toward its zenith overhead. Clouds began to gather in the east, piling up in fluffy thunderheads. Crows squawked harshly overhead.

With the trail pointing this way, there were only two possible destinations: the Forks, a settlement fifty miles away where the Fortress River joined the Little Bear, or Outlaw Canyon, where the Taskers lived. If the rustler was headed for the Forks, catching him was only a matter of time. But if he was headed for Outlaw Canyon, he might not be caught at all. Unless Matt was prepared to ride into the canyon after him.

Noon came and passed, and shortly afterward

the trail Matt followed turned in at the mouth of Outlaw Canyon.

He halted his horse momentarily, frowning. He knew the risk he took if he turned here. If the rustler was one of the Taskers, he probably wouldn't ride out alive.

He stared northward into the canyon fastnesses. From here to its upper end was all of twenty miles. He could see the rims that walled it in even though they were twenty miles away. Out here, near the canyon mouth, the benches were rocky, steep, strewn with boulders that had broken off the high rimrock and rolled down in ages past. An occasional cedar grew on these piles of rock but that was all. A man might climb through them but not a horse.

He'd probably be watched from the time he entered the canyon mouth. He'd probably be stopped or turned back by rifle fire before he had gone a mile.

His eyes hardened slightly. His mouth thinned out. He spurred his horse. He entered the canyon mouth along a narrow road that paralleled the sluggish creek.

He held the horse to a steady gallop, never leaving the road. Heat seemed held in here, trapped by the high benches on either side, reflected upon the road by the rocky slopes. He could see dust settling ahead of him now and knew that he was very close.

At any time a rifle might speak from somewhere in the rocks. He knew he should turn back. Instead he kept on. And a few moments later he thundered around a shoulder of solid rock fifty feet high and saw five steers in the road ahead of him.

They were Fortress steers. He could see Fortress's earmark on each of them. But no horseman was visible.

Caution told him to turn around. Loyalty to Fortress and to old Chris told him that he must, at least, recover the stolen steers. He touched his horse's sides with his heels and moved forward.

He saw the rustler's horse at almost the same instant, standing quietly in some rocks in the bed of the creek. He heard the metallic sound of a rifle's action being opened and closed.

He flung himself from his horse instantly. As he touched the ground, he heard the rifle's roar.

He dived behind a rock, prone when he struck the ground. He wriggled farther behind its doubtful protection and tried to see from which vantage point the shot had come.

He spotted the powder smoke, drifting lazily away on still air. He ducked his head as a second bullet struck the rock behind which he lay.

But his quick glance had showed him more than the cloud of powder smoke. It had showed him his horse, lying motionless on its side.

The first bullet, then, had struck the horse. He turned his head and looked toward the canyon mouth. If he tried to make it afoot, he'd be exposed to the hidden rifleman. And there was no other way to get out of here.

His mouth twisted wryly. He'd gotten himself into it this time all right.

The rifle roared again, this time showering him with dirt. And this time he noticed how the report reverberated and echoed back and forth from canyon wall to canyon wall until it sounded like half a dozen shots instead of only one.

He shrugged fatalistically. He only had two choices and neither of them was very palatable. He could break from this skimpy cover and try to rush the rifleman. Or he could wait for dark.

Rushing the rustler was a risky business and he was almost sure to get shot before he reached the man. Waiting for dark wasn't much better because before then the rustler would have reinforcements from the Tasker ranch farther up the canyon. They could work their way behind him and when they did he would have no protection at all.

He scowled angrily. The rifle spoke again and this time the slug tore a rowel off one of his spurs and flung it, clanging, against the rocks behind him. He yanked the numbed foot closer to him so that it would not be exposed.

He didn't dare raise his head. He knew the rustler had a bead on the place where it would appear.

He began to sweat heavily in the baking sun. His

throat grew dry. He wanted a smoke but didn't dare move enough to withdraw the makings from the pocket of his shirt.

He lay this way for a long, long time, his head against the ground. Through it, as vibrations, he heard the approach of several horses on the hard-packed road.

Knowing his time had nearly run out, he risked poking his head out to the side of the rock. The rifle roared almost immediately, but the bullet, because of the marksman's sudden change of aim, missed.

Matt whistled softly to himself. He had thought perhaps he could reach the rustler's horse, but his quick glance had showed him how impossible it was. The horse was fifty yards away. There was little or no cover between the horse and the place where he lay.

He might as well face the truth. He had ridden into a situation from which there was no escape. Death was only minutes away.

He put his ear to the ground again. The horsemen were closer now. He'd see them coming around that bend in the road very soon.

He raised his head as much as he dared, and watched the road. He saw the cattle raise their heads. He saw them turn to run. And then he saw Wiley, Court and Floyd Tasker come riding down the road.

He yelled, "Floyd! If you don't want to be

charged with rustlin' yourselves, you'd better flush that thief out of the rocks over there!"

His answer was a rifle bullet from across the creek, one that ricocheted from the rock behind which he lay and whined away into space.

The Taskers swung from their horses. One swung his rifle toward Matt while the other two walked toward the hidden rifleman. Matt heard Court say, "Wes!"

He supposed he had known it was Wes all along but until now he hadn't admitted it. He heard Wes shout, "Spread out and get the sonofabitch! He isn't going to charge anybody with anything because he isn't getting out of here!"

There seemed to be an argument going on. For several moments Matt heard their low-pitched voices though he could not distinguish their words. At last Wes yelled, "Get him, damn it! If you don't maybe I'll tell him how many Fortress cattle have come up this road in the last six months!"

Matt ducked as Floyd Tasker, standing in the road, raised his gun and fired. He saw Tasker begin to run for the cover of some rocks.

He yanked his revolver, risking exposure to Wes, and snapped a shot at the man. But Tasker made it to the rocks untouched.

Matt was now flanked, and probably exposed. He heard the sounds of running boots as the other two Taskers ran downcountry to flank him from that side.

His body was soaked with sweat. He tensed his muscles, preparatory to getting up. If he had to die, he wasn't going to do it like a mole in a burrow or a rattler hiding behind a rock. He'd die on his feet like a man at least.

And then, as his head momentarily touched the ground, he heard vibrations that could only mean the approach of another horse.

Was it the old man, father of Wiley and Court and Floyd? Was it old Ben Tasker, coming to help them out? Or was it someone else, perhaps someone coming from the other direction, from the mouth of the canyon to the south?

He held his ear tightly against the ground. One horse. No more than that. Then it certainly wasn't help for Matt.

He raised his head. As he did, a rider thundered around the bend, scattering the cattle which were on the road again. The rider came on, to haul up immediately beside Matt's dead horse.

He heard Floyd's voice, "Josie! Damn it, you get out of here before you get shot!"

Josie shouted worriedly, "Matt?" Her voice was filled with fright. He supposed she recognized his saddle, though she couldn't have seen it more than half a dozen times.

He didn't reply, because Floyd was right. She could catch a stray bullet if he got up.

She cried, "Matt! Are you hurt?"

The shooting had stopped. He realized suddenly

that she was between Wes and himself. He also realized that her brothers wouldn't shoot, nor would they let Wes shoot, if there was the slightest chance she would be hit.

This was the only chance he had. He got up suddenly and sprinted toward her.

Her eyes widened slightly but she held her frightened horse still. He saw Wes across the creek, his rifle raised. He heard Floyd yell, "Wes! Damn you, if you shoot—"

Then he reached her and heard her urgent, "Get up behind me. They won't shoot because they're afraid of hitting me."

He vaulted to the saddle behind her. Her spurs dug in and her frightened horse plunged away down the road. There were two shots behind them—warning shots fired at Wes, he guessed—and then all was still.

CHAPTER 5

Her body was slight and warm against his own. The wind of their own creation whipped her long red hair back into his face, and it was as fragrant as spring.

A deep, copper color now. Not bright, brick red as it once had been. He could see one side of her face, an ear, and part of her straight, slender neck. She turned her face and for an instant her startling green eyes met his own. "Are you all right, Matt?"

He nodded wordlessly, suddenly unable to talk. After a moment he swallowed and said, "You sure saved my neck, but you'll catch it when you get back."

"I'm not afraid of them."

Again there was silence between them, but he remained very conscious of her. His arm, around her waist, tightened briefly and he saw color stain her cheek.

They reached the mouth of the canyon and she put her horse straight into the river. In the middle, where the horse was forced to swim, Matt slipped from the saddle and, hanging onto a stirrup leather, let the horse tow him along. When the horse regained his footing on the other side, Matt pulled himself back onto its broad, wet rump.

They splashed out of the river and were lost in

the brush and trees on the other side. They began to climb.

Josie turned her head once and said, "I'd better take you all the way. If I don't, they'll hunt you down."

Matt nodded. The sun was getting low in the west. He knew it would be dark long before they reached home. He said, "If we should see some Fortress horses I could catch one up."

"If we see any." There seemed to be an odd strain in her voice. She would turn her head part way whenever she spoke, but she would not look directly at him.

He said softly, "It's been a long time, Josie."

"Yes." There seemed to be a certain rigidity in her body that had not been there before. He asked, "How have you been?"

"I've been all right. Why wouldn't I be?"

"I've thought about you."

She turned her head and for the first time looked steadily into his eyes. Her own eyes snapped. "Not very often, I'll bet."

He said, "You're pretty, Josie. You're not a little girl any more."

"Don't you make fun of me."

"I'm not making fun of you." His arm around her waist tightened again. She said, "You're getting me all wet." But there was a catch in her voice and no anger at all.

The horse labored up the steep slope, through

high sagebrush that left a pungent smell in the air as the horse's hoofs crushed it, through equally high greasewood, sarvus and scrub oak. At last, high on the slope, they reached the fragrant pines.

Matt hipped around and stared down at the river valley far below. Josie stopped the horse, lathered from the climb and breathing hard.

Matt slipped to the ground. He put up his hand to her but she ignored it and dismounted by herself. She asked, almost breathlessly, "See them coming?"

He stared, squinting against the brilliant rays of the setting sun. There was dust down there but it was between the river and the mouth of the canyon. He saw four tiny specks riding toward the canyon mouth and said, "They've given up. They're going back."

They were in shadow now. The sun was behind the ridge on which they stood. Matt shivered.

Josie untied the blanket roll from behind her saddle. "Get out of that wet shirt and put these blankets over you."

He took off the shirt and hung it on the branch of a tree. Josie glanced at him once, her color heightening, and after that kept her eyes downcast. She handed him a blanket and he draped it over his shoulders and drew it closed in front. He spread the other one and sat down on it.

Josie sat down beside him and began trying to

pull off her boots. They were wet and filled with water and try as she would, she couldn't get them off. He said, "Let me help."

He stood up and took hold of one of the boots. He pulled, but only succeeded in skidding Josie along the ground.

He turned around, holding her foot between his legs. "Put your other foot against me."

She did. He worked the boot back and forth and at last it came off. He released her sodden foot and she put it against his rump while he pulled the other boot. It came loose more suddenly than the first, throwing him forward, staggering. He lost his balance and sprawled on the carpet of pine needles underfoot.

Josie laughed. He turned his head and grinned at her. Then his face sobered. He got up, walked back and stood over her, looking down.

Her own laugh died, but her eyes didn't leave his own. He sat down, the blanket gone from his shoulders. He was no longer cold. The blood seemed to be racing wildly through him and his skin seemed to burn.

Josie laid back on the blanket, still holding his glance with her own. Matt said, "Josie."

She did not reply. Her color was high and there was a strange expression in her eyes, one he had never seen there before. He turned toward her. Her hands came up and touched his chest as lightly as a vagrant breeze. Her lips were parted and her breasts rose and fell rapidly. Her breath was warm and sweet in his nostrils.

Suddenly his mouth was against hers, harshly, demandingly, urgently. Her arms went around his neck and her body moved closer to his own until it burned along the entire length of him.

He drew away, murmuring, "Josie, Josie."

He buried his face in her throat, his hands fumbling with the buttons on her blouse. It came open and her naked breasts were warm and soft against his chest.

High overhead ravens wheeled and squalled, unheard by the two on the soft carpet of pine needles far below. Gold stained the clouds and faded as dusk slipped quietly over the empty land. And at last darkness flowed down the timbered slopes, and enveloped the pair lying motionless and spent at last.

Her face was against his jaw, her breath mingling sweetly with his own. One of her arms lay across his chest. She almost seemed to be sleeping, but he knew she was not when she said in a small, scared voice, "What happened to us, Matt? Why—"

"I don't know, Josie. I couldn't stop myself. I'm sorry."

"Sorry? Why are you sorry, Matt?" She raised herself to an elbow and peered down at him in the gathering dark.

He was silent, gathering his thoughts, wanting

to tell her exactly what he felt: that what had happened wasn't fair to her, but it was more to him, much more, than a passing incident; that he loved her, perhaps, though he had never told a girl that in his life and wasn't sure he could right now.

She misunderstood his silence. Her voice was tight and strained when she spoke again, and she pulled coldly away from him. "You needn't worry, Matt. I won't try and force you to marry me."

She yanked on her boots, got to her feet, snatched up her blouse and put it on. She made a vague, blurred shape in the darkness and the catch in her voice told him she was near to tears.

He got quickly to his feet. "I didn't mean that, Josie."

"Don't lie, Matt. Don't make it worse by lying to me."

"I'm not lying. Damn it—"

"There's no need to swear. Just because I'm a Tasker doesn't mean—"

"Tasker? What the hell's that got to do with anything?"

"Please Matt. Don't shout at me."

"Shout at you? I'll do more than that if I have to. You're going to listen to me!"

She darted away from him. "Don't touch me, Matt. Don't touch me again!" Her voice broke and he could hear her crying softly less than twenty feet away from him.

"Josie, listen to me. Please!"

"It's no use, Matt. I just wish—"

He heard stirrup leather creak as she swung to her horse's back. She was crying openly now. He ran toward her, to catch her horse and keep her from riding off.

His foot caught on an exposed tree root and he fell headlong. Her horse started and plunged away.

Matt lay prone, cursing softly to himself. The hoofbeats of Josie's horse gradually died away and disappeared.

When would he see her again, and how? She never came to town and even if she did it was always in the company of one or more of her brothers, who watched her all the time. He certainly couldn't ride into Outlaw Canyon to see her—not after what had happened.

Standing now in the huge living room at Fortress Ranch, he realized that he hadn't seen her, except at a distance, since that day. He hadn't talked to her. He'd had no opportunity to tell her how he really felt about that day, that it was one of his sweetest memories.

He realized he was pacing nervously back and forth. His jaws had been clenched so long they ached.

He'd walked all the way home from where she'd left him that night, worried about her and about what her brothers would do to her when she returned home, unable to do anything about it and keenly feeling his helplessness.

He arrived at Fortress in the early hours of the morning, footsore, exhausted, hungry and out of sorts. The cook had coffee going and he drank three cups while he waited for the cook to fix him something to eat.

And all the time he cursed himself for being a fool. He should have spoken up immediately when he realized that Josie had misunderstood. He should have *made* her believe him. But he hadn't and it was too late to change that now.

He walked across the room, got a bottle of whisky from behind a shelf of books and poured himself a drink. He gulped it and poured another. He gulped that one too.

The liquor warmed him but it didn't drive away his hopelessness. Tomorrow he would ride to town. He would get the sheriff and a posse and ride with them and the Fortress crew into Outlaw Canyon. The Taskers' rustling days were over.

Some of them, perhaps all of them, would be killed, along with many members of the posse and Fortress's crew. Josie would hate him when she knew he was responsible, even if she didn't hate him now.

It hurt him to realize that there was now no chance of ever holding her in his arms again. There was no chance that she would lie beside him in the night, and bear his children. . . .

He looked at the tall clock standing against the wall. It was almost midnight. If he didn't get some sleep he wouldn't be fit to ride to town after the sheriff tomorrow, let alone lead his crew and a posse into Outlaw Canyon.

The force of the wind had diminished. It was still raining, but less violently. He went through the kitchen and stepped onto the wide back porch of the house.

There was a smell in the air, a clean, washed smell of pines, and earth, and wet wood. And there was a fresh coolness too that suddenly reminded him of fall.

Rain dripped steadily from the eaves and made a softer patter falling out in the bare ranch yard. Again he told himself he ought to go to bed, but he didn't go. He was still remembering—remembering Chris's face when he had told him of the five stolen steers and told him who the thief had been. Remembering that Chris's face had showed pain but no surprise. He had realized then that Chris had known all the time that Wes was stealing from him. But Chris hadn't known, or hadn't been willing to admit even to himself, that Wes was capable of killing someone practically a member of his own household.

Hope died in Chris that day. He stopped deluding himself that Wes would change. He resigned himself to the inevitable, which was that eventually Wes would either go to prison or hang. He stopped thinking he could stop the frightening march of destiny.

And when hope died in him, he began dying a little each day physically. Matt watched that too, with growing anger at Wes, with increasing hopelessness in himself.

Chris stopped riding the wide miles of Fortress range. He refused to eat and lost interest in everything.

Matt did the best he could. When Chris fired the foreman for calling Wes a few well-chosen and well-deserved names, Matt took over and tried to run Fortress the way he knew Chris would want it run.

He could hold Fortress together, but he couldn't do the same for Chris. However he wanted to and however he tried, he couldn't stop the disintegration of Chris's body and mind.

CHAPTER 6

He never stopped trying, though. That fall, after Matt's promotion to foreman, Chris wanted him to ride the caboose to Denver with Fortress's cattle train. Matt refused unless Chris went along. Reluctantly and a little angrily, Chris finally agreed. And that was how Odie Hendrix came into Chris's life. . . .

Matt frowned lightly and stepped out into the yard. The rain fell softly, lightly on his bare head and upturned face. The ground was muddy underfoot, but the warm rain felt good to him. For some reason it seemed to calm his thoughts.

Thoughts about Odie were not usually calm. Chris and Matt met her at the hotel. She was a widow and though she had never told either of them her exact age, Matt judged she was about thirty-five.

She was a full-bodied woman, a warm woman, with a softness about her that stirred Chris almost instantly. Her hair was a warm brown and so were her eyes. Her mouth was full, usually smiling, and a plain bridge of freckles spanned her nose. There was a rare and natural charm to her and she seemed to know what Chris needed and seemed able to give it to him.

Matt liked her and so did Chris. They'd sit at dinner with her in the hotel dining room and her eyes would sparkle as she carried the conversation alone, making both of them feel at ease, soon bringing them to laughter over some story she had told.

And Chris began to disappear with her. They took early morning rides in a rented buggy. Once or twice they drove all the way to the mountains for a picnic lunch.

Chris would grin sheepishly at Matt when he returned, and Matt would poke good-natured fun at him about his "widow girl." But Chris began to take interest in his appearance again. And Matt was glad to see the change in him.

He understood what all this was leading up to, whether Chris did yet or not. And so, one night after Chris returned, Matt left the room and went down the hall to Odie's room.

He knocked lightly on the door, feeling clumsy and awkward, feeling as though he was interfering where he had no right to interfere. Yet stubbornly he stayed until Odie answered the door. Matt knew Chris had been hurt enough. He wanted to be sure Odie wouldn't hurt him too.

"Why Matt! What on earth are you doing here at this time of night?"

"I want to talk to you."

She studied him, flushing a little, doubt visible in her eyes. He said hastily, "I want to talk to you about Chris. We could go downstairs—"

"Of course we won't go downstairs. You come right in."

He went in. Her room was filled with frilly women's things and apparently it was her permanent residence. He said bluntly, "Chris thinks a lot of you. I have an idea that before we leave he's going to ask you to marry him."

She flushed faintly. "He already has."

"And what was your answer?"

"I haven't given him one." Her brown eyes, so steady and calm, were reassuring to Matt.

He said, "Has he told you anything about himself?"

"He never talks about himself. Sometimes he talks about his ranch, but never about himself."

"He's never told you about Wes?"

She shook her head.

"Then maybe I'd better." Matt told her about Wes, about how Chris had been hurt by him. He told her what it had done to Chris and that he had only begun to come to life again under her influence. He said determinedly as he finished, "I don't want to see him hurt again."

"Why I wouldn't hurt him, Matt!"

"Are you going to marry him?"

She nodded. "I think so."

"Why? Are you in love with him?"

She met his glance honestly and shook her head. "No, but I think I can keep him from knowing that." She glanced down and said, "I'll be honest, Matt. I guess I want the things Chris can give to me. I want security. A widow's life is not a pleasant one and I have no money of my own. But I think I can give him something in return." Again she raised her eyes to him. "I know I'm going to try very, very hard."

Matt took her hand and squeezed it lightly. He smiled. "That's good enough for me."

If only he'd understood Odie better, he thought, it might have changed what came afterward. Or maybe it wouldn't have changed anything.

They stayed on in Denver two weeks more. And when they did return, they brought Odie Hendrix along as Chris's wife.

She'd promised Matt she'd do her best to make Chris forget the troubles he'd had with Wes. And she quite obviously tried very hard to do just that. And then one day Odie drove the buggy to town by herself and there she ran into Wes.

Matt never understood what it was about Wes that so attracted her. Perhaps, physically at least, Wes was Chris as a younger man. Perhaps by then she was beginning to regret the bargain she had made with Chris. He was much older than she. And life at Fortress was, in its way, a lonely and unexciting one. Odie didn't like to ride. She had no interest in nature or in the operations of the ranch. She was afraid of cattle and of the emptiness of the land.

Odie was like Mary in that respect, though she didn't fear it as much as Mary had. But she spent practically all of her time alone in the big house—

until she met Wes and began driving to town two or three times every week.

Matt didn't realize what was going on at first and neither did Chris. But one day Matt rode to town to pick up an urgently needed mower part. And he saw Odie meeting Wes.

Mesa was not a large town. It boasted, in all, ninety-seven inhabitants. In addition, there were usually a few drifters temporarily in town, and daytimes, a scattering of punchers and ranch folk, in for supplies or mail.

It had but three streets in all. Main, which held the business houses and two saloons, First, a block west and Third, a block east of Main. First and Third were lined with residences for the entire two-block length of the town.

Matt rode in just as Odie came out of Roark's Mercantile. She got into her buggy and drove away—not toward Fortress but away from it.

Matt dismounted at the rail in front of Roark's and started to loop his reins. Then he stopped. Half a block away he saw Wes detach himself from the wall of the saloon and mount his horse. Wes rode out of town in the wake of the buggy, staying about half a block behind but plainly following it.

Matt frowned. He watched for several minutes, scoffing at himself for the suspicions running through his mind. It wasn't unnatural for Odie to come to town two or three times a week. She was bored and lonely on the ranch. Just because Wes happened to ride out of town at almost the same time didn't mean anything.

But she wasn't heading toward home—and if Wes would steal his father's cattle it wasn't too farfetched to believe he might also steal his father's wife.

Matt turned and kicked the veranda step disgustedly. It was getting so. . . . He started up the steps to the open front door of the store. And then he stopped again. Chris had been hurt enough. If what he was thinking was true, Chris would be hurt again—even more than he had been hurt before. This would finish him.

Abruptly Matt turned and went back down the steps. He swung to the back of his horse. Moving at a slow, deliberate walk, he rode out of town.

Both the buggy and Wes had disappeared. So Matt kept his gaze on the ground and followed the buggy tracks. Occasionally he looked up, glancing warily ahead.

He felt sneaky and mean, until he remembered how Wes had once spied on him and Josie Tasker at the school. After that he had no qualms. Besides, he was thinking of Chris too.

He traveled about two miles before he found where the buggy had turned off into a grove of willows bordering the river. Thereafter he rode more slowly and carefully, because the tracks of a horse had turned off at the same place the buggy had. And because he knew how Wes hated him.

The feeling of nausea in Matt's stomach grew when he saw the buggy directly ahead of him, the buggy horse tied to a tree. Wes's horse was tied immediately beside it.

Matt swung to the ground. Moving as silently and as carefully as an Indian, he followed Odie's tracks from the buggy into the underbrush. It was obvious to him now that this was a regular tryst, that both of them knew where it was and went to it familiarly.

He traveled silenty for about three hundred yards. And then he heard Odie's laugh ahead of him.

He had found out what he wanted to know. He knew he should go back. But suddenly his fury was too great for that. He wanted to kill Wes and Odie too.

No longer did he move with stealth. He charged ahead like an angry bull. He burst into a tiny clearing. The faces of both turned toward him and the eyes of both grew wide with surprise and fear. Odie's hands were fumbling frantically with the front of her blouse, trying to get it closed.

Matt yelled, "You goddam bitch! Chasing off into the bushes with another man is bad enough, but did it have to be his son?"

Her face, white at first, now flushed painfully. Matt turned his blazing glance on Wes. "How rotten can you get? First you steal cattle from him! Now you steal his wife!"

The surprise had gone from Wes's face. It was suddenly angry, both with frustration and, Matt supposed, with guilt.

Wes's gun and belt lay on the grass where he and Odie had been lying when they heard Matt's approach. He glanced at it, then glanced back at Matt.

Matt said flatly, "Go ahead. Try for it. I just wish you would. I wouldn't kill you that night in the saloon, but by God I'll kill you now! Go ahead. Grab your goddam gun!"

Some of the anger faded from Wes's eyes to be replaced by fear. Matt said disgustedly, "Then kick it over here."

Wes hooked the gunbelt with a boot toe, not looking at it. He kicked it toward Matt and Matt picked it up. He said, "Don't see her again. If you do, I'll kill you with my two bare hands!"

He glanced at Odie. "Fix your clothes and go on home."

She stumbled away, face blazing and eyes downcast. Matt waited until he heard the iron tires of the buggy grate on a rock as they rolled over it.

He turned and walked through the underbrush to his horse. He was sick inside with anger and with helplessness. This was a thing he would never, could never tell Chris. This must be kept from the old man no matter what the cost.

He mounted his horse. He rode slowly, letting the buggy stay well ahead of him. In town, he stopped and picked up the part for which he had come, then continued toward Fortress, still following the buggy tracks . . .

Standing here now in Fortress's yard, pelted by gentle, warm rain, Matt's body suddenly burned with rage, as he remembered what had happened next.

Odie's lovemaking must have been something, because Wes hadn't been able to stay away from her. Matt came back two weeks later from a two-day swing around Fortress's range to find Wes and a friend, Rudy Olguin, living at the ranch.

Chris's eyes had glowed as he told Matt about it. "He's come home, Matt! He's come home to stay! He's sorry for all the things he's done and he's going to change. And I think he will. I think he can, now. You don't know how much this means to me, Matt. You just don't know how much it means!"

Matt clamped his jaws shut tight. He looked at Chris's shining eyes and knew he couldn't say a thing. He'd have to keep silent, knowing what was going on, unable to stop it or to drive Wes away.

He'd come very close to going away himself that night, but he hadn't been able to. He knew violence was coming to Fortress Ranch, violence that would involve them all. He couldn't bring himself to leave Chris to face it all alone.

Rudy Olguin was an undersized man with a narrow, expressionless face. His legs were slightly bowed from riding, but he never rode a horse if he had a choice. He preferred a buggy, a buckboard, even a wagon to a horse.

He dressed much as Wes did, and it was not long before Matt understood that Wes had patterned his own dress after that of Olguin.

Olguin wore his gun low slung and tied down with a leather thong above his knee. The weathered holster and exposed gun made an incongruous note against the background of his otherwise conservative attire.

Rudy's eyes were a light tan color and always gave the impression of looking through you instead of at you. He was a killer, a professional. He would kill for a hundred dollars. He often had, if his stories were to be believed, and Matt believed the stories.

Every day Rudy took a couple of boxes of shells for his revolver and walked half a mile away from the house in the direction of the towering hulk of Fortress Mesa. If the wind was right, Matt would sometimes hear the popping of his gun and the echos bouncing back from the mesa's sheer cliffs. Once he rode within sight of Rudy, and watched him, and was amazed at the eye-blurring speed of his gun.

Olguin stayed in the house, in the room next to Wes's room, which was just across the hall from

Odie's room. She had pleaded to Chris that she did not sleep well in a double bed and so had obtained his consent to sleep in a separate room.

A convenient arrangement for both her and Wes, Matt had thought sourly. Just so Chris didn't find out what was going on.

He didn't either, for seven long months. But the night he did would always remain in Matt's memory like a sharp and stabbing pain.

He doubted if he would ever really know exactly what happened on the second floor of the house at Fortress that awful night. He doubted if anyone really knew but Chris, and Chris either couldn't or wouldn't talk about it. But Matt knew enough.

He was sleeping in the bunkhouse, in the same bunk in which he'd slept since coming to Fortress so many years before. It was early spring and the bunkhouse doors were open to the warm spring night. A breeze blew up off the river at the foot of the benches, carrying with it a dank but not unpleasant smell. A few early crickets chirped in the cottonwoods surrounding the house.

From a sound sleep, Matt was yanked rudely to consciousness by a woman's scream. He sat bolt upright, stunned with such sudden awakening. Somewhere in the bunkhouse a hoarse, sleepy voice muttered, "Holy Christ! What the hell was that?"

Matt swung his feet over the edge of his bunk. He stood up and pulled on his pants. Before he could reach for his boots, he heard the scream again.

Shrill, filled with a stark terror that put chills into Matt's spine, it stopped suddenly as though cut off.

He didn't take time for his boots. Something in him, some caution that perhaps remembered that both Wes and Rudy Olguin were in the house, made him snatch his gun and belt from a nail as he went past the foot of his bunk. Then he was out the door and running for the house as fast as he could go.

Why he ran for the front door instead of for the back, he would never know. He could hear other feet pounding along behind him as other crew members, awakened by the scream, followed him. He finished strapping on his gun and belt as he reached the house and flung the door open and plunged inside.

It was utterly black and he couldn't see a thing. But he could hear sound. He could hear sounds not quite human, that increased the chills and coldness traveling along his spine. Reason told him those sounds were human; logic told him they came from a human throat, too closed with rage and shock and grief to utter normal sounds.

He stood motionless for a moment, during which some member of the crew struck a match and lighted a nearby lamp.

Odie lay, naked and still, at the bottom of the

stairs. In the shadows at the head of them, Matt could see Chris, standing like a statue, his mouth moving, his throat in convulsion, but no words coming out.

Matt snatched up an Indian blanket from a sofa as he crossed the room and covered Odie with it. He knelt beside her and picked up her hand. He felt her wrist for pulse.

There was no pulse. He noticed then that her head lay at an odd angle to the rest of her.

He went slowly up the stairs. That which he had so feared had happened at last. The look on Chris's face told him that. He reached the old man, who was clad in a nightshirt and said, "Come on, Chris. Come back to bed and I'll get you a drink."

Chris let himself be led along the darkened hall. Inside his bedroom, Matt struck a match and lighted a lamp. Chris sat down numbly on the edge of the bed.

Matt went to the dresser, where a bottle and glass stood. He pulled the cork and poured half a tumbler full. He handed it to Chris.

As he did he heard swift, stealthy footsteps in the hall and afterward on the stairs. Wes was leaving, then, and Olguin was leaving with him. He would go after them soon, but not until Chris had quieted down and gone to sleep.

CHAPTER 7

Chris remained seated numbly on the side of the bed. He gulped the whisky when Matt handed it to him. Matt got the bottle and poured some more. If he could load enough whisky into Chris, he'd have to go to sleep.

Chris drank another half tumbler as though it was water. He sat utterly still for a moment, hair tousled, face sweating heavily. Then his eyes rose and met those of Matt. His voice, though hoarse, was rational. "I caught 'em. I caught 'em in bed together an' not a stitch on either of 'em."

"Wes?"

Chris nodded.

Matt asked, "Did you kill her, Chris?"

Chris's eyes clouded. Matt seized his arms and shook him gently. "Did you Chris?"

"I don't know. I wanted to." He frowned as though trying to remember something that eluded him. "Someone ran past me and out the door."

"Odie or Wes?"

Chris didn't answer directly. He said numbly, "I went for her. I was going to kill her, Matt, and I guess I did."

Matt said, "Wait a minute now. Someone ran past you, you said. Was Odie still there afterward?"

"That's when I went for her."

70

"Wes ran out then. What happened after that?"

"I didn't get her. She got out of the other side of the bed and ran."

"Was that when she screamed?"

Chris nodded.

"The first time?"

Chris nodded again.

Matt stared at him. The only thing he could feel was pity and an overpowering desire to save Chris from any more pain. If he was forced to go on trial for the murder of his wife, that would be the end.

He got Chris another half tumbler of whisky. Then he said, "It was dark and she was scared. She ran out into that dark hall and fell down the stairs. It's as simple as that."

Chris didn't glance up. Matt suddenly didn't care how it really had happened. This was the story the world was going to get. If Chris had killed Odie he had certainly been justified.

Matt said sharply, "Chris, look at me. And listen. Remember what I say."

Chris looked up and met his eyes. Matt said, "You didn't kill her. She got away from you and ran. The hall was dark and she fell down the stairs. As she fell, she screamed a second time. It *was* that way, now wasn't it Chris?"

"It could have been, I guess." Chris looked puzzled and scared. "I don't remember, Matt. I don't remember a thing."

"Then that's the story the sheriff's going to get."

He could see the liquor beginning to take effect on Chris. He poured another half tumbler and handed it to him. Chris downed it in two gulps.

Matt blew out the lamp. "Go to sleep, Chris. I'll take care of everything."

He went out and closed the door. He heard the bed creak heavily as Chris lay back.

Matt went down the stairs. At the foot he knelt and gathered Odie's body up with the Indian blanket still covering it. He carried it upstairs and into her bedroom, where he laid it on the bed. He covered it without removing the Indian blanket and went back out into the hall. He went down the stairs.

Six crew members were standing uneasily in the living room. Matt said, "Larry, go get the sheriff and Doc Place. Mrs. Knudson fell down the stairs in the dark and broke her neck."

Larry turned to go. Matt said, "Wait."

Larry turned. Matt looked at their faces, one at a time. He said, "That's all there is to it, understand?"

All of them nodded vigorously. Matt asked, "Which way did Wes and Olguin go?"

"Toward the river, Matt. Probably to Outlaw's Canyon."

"Then that's where I'll be too."

He ran outside, crossed the yard and selected the fastest horse in the corral. He roped him, saddled him, and swung to his back. He thundered away recklessly.

He spurred the horse without mercy, unable at

times to see the ground but knowing the horse saw well enough. Outlaw's Canyon was not going to become a refuge for Wes—not this time—but his chances of getting his man would be better if he beat him to the canyon mouth.

He doubted if either Wes or Olguin would expect to be pursued. Not this soon at least.

Only when his horse faltered, did he allow the animal to slow and walk. The trail led ever down, through timber and heavy brush, and there were times when the horse slid on his haunches down some steep precipice.

The stars were fading as Matt reached the river valley directly below the ranch. He found the road, reined west, and spurred his horse again.

Several times the animal stumbled, from exhaustion, but not many more miles remained. And even if he killed the horse, Matt intended to be at the mouth of the canyon when Wes and Olguin arrived.

Dawn lightened the eastern sky, spreading gradually to encompass all of it. The rising sun stained the high clouds and, as Matt reached the canyon mouth, stained the high rims of Fortress Mesa orange. A hundred yards short of where he wished to go, his horse stumbled and fell headlong. Matt was catapulted forward, rolling.

He scrambled to his feet, hearing the approaching pound of hoofs. He ducked quickly behind a rock.

Wes and Olguin rode into sight, their horses wet from the river crossing. Matt stepped from behind the rock, his gun in his hand.

Olguin's hand streaked for his side, but Matt had the edge because his was already drawn. Its muzzle moved into line and the hammer fell. Smoke billowed from the muzzle. The report echoed back from the nearby canyon walls.

Olguin was driven sideways as his horse turned. He sprawled to the ground.

But Matt had no eyes for him now that his threat had been removed. He swung his gun toward Wes and fired a second time—fired just as Wes's horse reared in fright. His bullet struck the horse instead of Wes.

Wes spilled from the saddle and the horse narrowly missed falling on him. A cloud of dust arose.

As Matt moved his gun muzzle to follow Wes, Olguin fired at him from the ground. The bullet grazed his thigh, burning, drawing a sudden rush of blood.

His leg gave way and he spilled helplessly to the dust. He fought to bring his gun around.

Olguin fired again and again, but both shots missed. Matt could see blood streaming from Olguin's shoulder, soaking his torn shirt, the rent in which exposed the wound. Olguin's face was twisted . . .

Wes got up and ran, and disappeared into the

brush. Matt got up and followed, weaving, dodging, while Olguin emptied his gun at him. Neither Wes nor Matt now had a horse. But both were armed. Matt stopped, listened briefly until he heard the crashing sound of Wes's passage through the brush, then pounded in pursuit.

Neither was used to running. Neither had ever walked anywhere if he could ride a horse. Matt's breath played out and his chest burned furiously. He stopped, breathing raggedly, and waited until it calmed.

There was no sound ahead. But, two hundred yards away, he saw Wes start up the rocky slope.

He raised the gun and fired. The bullet struck a rock short of Wes and ricocheted away. Matt fired again and again the bullet was short. He shoved the gun into its holster and ran again.

Wes took two shots at him, then turned and continued to scramble hurriedly up the rocks. Matt reached the foot of them and started in pursuit.

He dodged a boulder as big as a buggy wheel that Wes rolled down on him, but half a dozen smaller rocks struck him. One hit him in the leg. One struck him in the forehead and drove him, momentarily stunned, to his knees.

He recovered and went on, panting, sweating heavily, dizzy from exertion and lack of air, knowing Wes was no better off than he.

It seemed to continue forever, this heedless,

infuriated pursuit. He forgot that he carried a gun. His hands began to bleed from clawing upward over the bare, unyielding rocks. His pants were torn and his knees were bleeding too.

And then, at last, the summit of the ridge loomed suddenly ahead. Wes stood there, half doubled, his breathing like a bellows. His gun was in his hand and steadying on Matt.

Matt snatched for his own holstered gun. His hand encountered only emptiness. Frantically he groped, then swung his head and stared behind. He saw no gun; he had lost it somewhere during the climb.

Wes's gun barked and the inner canyon walls picked up the sound and flung it back. The bullet struck a rock a foot away from Matt and whined away.

He plunged on recklessly. He couldn't remember how many times Wes had shot, but there couldn't be too many loads left in his gun. Wes fired again. Suddenly Matt remembered how many times Wes had shot at him. Twice as he started up the slope. Twice here. It meant only one bullet remained in Wes's gun.

Wes waited until Matt was less than a dozen yards away. Then he raised the gun and fired again.

This bullet took Matt in the fleshy part of the shoulder and half spun him around. But he didn't stop. He plunged on, grinning fiercely as he heard Wes's hammer click on an empty cylinder.

Wes flung the gun at him. He turned to run.

Matt dived at him and caught him by one ankle. He spilled Wes forward, skidding, in the rocks at the top of the ridge. As he clawed along the ground toward Wes, his eye caught sight of a horse beyond the ridge, pounding along that road that led into the canyon mouth. The rider had to be Olguin.

Wes rolled, kicking savagely. One of his boots caught Matt in the mouth. Then Matt reached him and slammed his head down against the crumbling rocks.

Wes's face was red, his eyes burning with both hatred and fear. He tried to knee Matt in the crotch and failed. Then he tried to get his thumbs into Matt's eyes.

Matt turned his head to avoid them. Wes broke free and scrambled to his feet. Matt got up and the two faced each other warily for a moment, both breathing hard.

Wes screeched hysterically, "God damn you, all my life you been right square in my way every time I wanted something! The old man gave you the best of everything right from the start! A freightyards bum! A dirty freightyards bum! I'm going to kill you if it's the last thing I ever do!"

Matt stared at his reddened eyes, at his mouth, twisting with his words as though he were near to tears. For an instant his hatred dimmed in the face of unwilling pity. Wes was about as twisted as a man could get. Chris had done everything for him, but Wes didn't believe he had. He never would believe it. Matt wondered suddenly if Mrs. Knudson hadn't borne too heavy a share of the blame for Wes all through the years. Maybe Wes alone was to blame. A man who is sure he's getting the dirty end of everything seldom gets disappointed. But he was dead wrong in one respect. Chris had never given him the dirty end of anything.

Matt moved toward him and Wes backed, a careful step at a time. As he did, he unbuckled his heavy, shell-laden gunbelt and looped it around his wrist.

Matt lunged. The gunbelt whistled as it swung. It took him squarely on the side of the head.

He shook his head groggily, but kept coming. The shellbelt swung again.

This time he was ready for it. It looped around his outstretched arm, and as it slid off he caught it with his hand and yanked.

Wes released it instantly, but not before he had been yanked bodily toward Matt. Matt dropped the belt and swung a savage right that landed solidly in the middle of Wes's face.

Wes's nose seemed to split. Blood spurted from both his nostrils. He staggered back and Matt followed him. His fists slammed into Wes regularly, with vicious accuracy. Wes's eyes glazed and he went down.

Eyes open but unseeing. Mouth open, drooling blood, gasping for lifegiving air.

Matt toed him with his boot. Wes's body gave yieldingly.

Matt cursed. He hadn't had enough. He hadn't finished with Wes but there was nothing more he could do right now. Disgustedly he turned and tramped back down the steep and rocky slope he had ascended with such difficulty only minutes ago.

It took but a few minutes to reach his horse, up on his feet and grazing now. He swung to the saddle groggily. He turned the horse toward home, letting him choose his own course, his own slow pace.

He had not given Wes what he deserved, but he had done the best he could. Now it was time to go home and see how old Chris was.

CHAPTER 8

It was past noon when Matt reached the ranch. He rode in and dismounted at the bunkhouse, before which a group of Fortress punchers had gathered. He handed his reins wearily to one of them. The man asked, "Catch 'em Matt?"

He nodded. "Olguin's got a bullet in him."

"What about Wes?"

"I didn't kill him, if that's what you mean. Put the horse away."

He tramped to the house and went in through the kitchen door. Benny Franks, the cook, glanced around at him. "Want somethin' to eat, Matt?"

Matt nodded. "And bring me some coffee, will you, Benny?"

"Sure. Doc Place is in there. Better get him to look at you. There's blood all over you."

"I'm all right." He went into the living room. Doc was there and so was Sherm Logan, the sheriff.

Doc Place was grizzled and elderly. He was the shortest man Matt knew, standing scarcely more than five feet. His body was blocky and beginning to grow a little fat. He looked up at Matt's face and said, "Sit down Matt. Lemme look at you. I guess those bullet holes ain't too bad or you wouldn't be on your feet. But they ought to be cleaned out and bandaged up. You've lost a lot of blood, looks like."

"How's Chris?" He sat down on the sofa and began to take off his shirt. Doc found some scissors in his bag and began to slit his trouser leg. He said, "I gave him something to make him sleep."

"Is he all right?"

"Rational you mean? Yeah, he's all right. But he's too old for a shock like this."

Matt glanced at the sheriff. "Did he tell you what happened?"

"A little of it. But I'd like to hear it again from you."

Matt nodded. He looked at Doc as he asked, "How about her? Is she—"

"I sent her body to town. Hope that was right."

Matt glanced at the sheriff. "I guess there's no use trying to hide anything, but I'd appreciate it and so would Chris if you'd keep what happened to yourself."

"As much as I can, Matt. You know that."

"Chris caught her in bed with Wes. She ran out into that dark hall and fell down the stairs. I heard her scream and ran in here. She was lying at the bottom of the stairs with her neck broken."

"Where was Chris?"

"Still in the bedroom," Matt lied.

"And Wes?"

Matt permitted himself a sour grin. "Getting dressed just as goddam fast as he could. He and

Olguin left while I was in Chris's room trying to pour enough whisky into him to make him sleep."

Logan stared at him speculatively. Matt winced as Doc began to clean the leg wound with alcohol. The sheriff asked, "Who shot you?"

"Olguin once. Wes gave me the other one."

"And them?"

"Olguin's got a hole in him but I don't think it's much worse than these. Last I saw of him he was riding up the road into Outlaw Canyon."

"What about Wes?"

"He'll heal."

"Want to swear out warrants for 'em?"

Matt glanced at the sheriff quizzically. "Would you ride into the canyon to serve 'em?"

Logan flushed. "That wasn't necessary Matt."

"No, I guess not. But somebody's going to have to go in there one of these days. It's getting so they think they can do anything and be safe as soon as they reach the canyon."

"It'd take an army."

"Then maybe we'd better go get an army."

"Maybe. But the evidence will have to be pretty goddam plain."

"It will be when I ask you to go in there."

Doc finished bandaging his leg and started on his arm. Matt knew how lucky he was. Either one of those bullets could have smashed a bone and crippled him for life. He was beginning to feel dizzy.

Logan, medium-sized, red-faced and cold of eye, said, "Doc and I have been talking about it. We think there ought to be an inquest."

"And let all that stuff come out?"

"Maybe it's better if it does come out. Otherwise, there's going to be a lot of whispering. First thing you know, people are liable to get the notion that Chris pushed her down those stairs. If the whole thing is aired now maybe that kind of talk will never get started."

Matt glanced up at him. "Are you just suggesting an inquest or have you already decided there's going to be one?"

"We've decided."

Matt shrugged, and winced. "All right. I won't fight you. But make it as easy for Chris as you can."

"Sure." This was Doc, just finishing with the bandages. "We don't want to hurt Chris any more than you do, Matt. He's been hurt enough. If I'd been him I'd have killed her an' Wes too. The sonofabitch!"

Matt asked, "When will it be?"

"Tomorrow morning at ten. Will you bring Chris in?"

"Uh-huh. We'll be there. And Doc—can you arrange for the funeral to be right afterward?"

Doc grunted assent. The sheriff said, "Be sure and bring those men who ran in here last night when you did. They'll have to testify."

Matt nodded and walked to the door with them. Doc got up into his buggy and Sherm Logan mounted his horse. Doc drove out of the yard, with Sherm following. Benny called Matt and, though he wasn't hungry now, he went out into the kitchen and ate. Afterwards he climbed the stairs and looked in at Chris's door. The old man lay on his back, mouth open, snoring. Matt closed the door. He stumbled down the hall to the room Wes had occupied, went in and sprawled face downward across the bed. Sleep hit him like a sledgehammer.

He did not awake until dawn the next day. He got up, wincing with the pains in his arm and leg. He felt as though he had been on a monstrous drunk.

He made a cigarette, then stumbled downstairs and into the kitchen. He went outside and put his head under the pump. He came back in and accepted the coffee Benny handed him.

He heard footsteps and turned his head. Chris Knudson stood in the doorway. Matt said, "Mornin', Chris."

"Hello Matt. What happened yesterday?"

"Nothing much, Chris. Nobody's hurt too bad."

"Did you go after them?"

Matt nodded. "I guess I lost my head."

"Wes ain't hurt, is he?"

"A few bruises is all."

Chris tried to smile. "I'm a fool, Matt. But he's still my son."

"Sure he is."

Benny gave Chris some coffee and returned to the stove. He began to fry flapjacks. The kitchen filled with their savory odor.

Matt said, "The inquest is this morning at ten. The funeral's right afterward."

Chris nodded without speaking. Benny silently brought them their breakfast and as silently they ate it. Chris got up. "I'll go get ready."

Matt went outside into the yard. He crossed to the bunkhouse and found the men who had run into the house with him the night Odie died. He said, "The sheriff wants all of you at the inquest. Get ready and saddle up."

He went out and crossed the yard. He caught a buggy horse, led him across the yard and hitched him in the buggy shafts. He drove the buggy to the house, got down and snapped the weight to the horse's bridle.

He went to the bunkhouse and changed his clothes. By the time he finished, Chris was waiting for him on the porch. The old man climbed to the buggy seat. Matt followed suit and picked up the reins.

The hands who were going with them fell in behind the buggy as it creaked out of the yard. Matt said, "I told the sheriff I found you in the bedroom after the accident."

"You think I pushed her, Matt?"

"Don't you remember?"

85

"No."

Matt said, "I don't think you pushed her but you sure had plenty of justification if you had. I just think it'd be better all around if you tell 'em you never left the bedroom until I got there."

"All right."

After that, Chris stared moodily ahead, not seeming to see anything. They reached Mesa and Matt pulled up in front of the courthouse. He got down and snapped on the weight. The hands tied their horses on either side of the buggy. Solemnly they filed inside.

Doc Place was county coroner. He sat up front at a desk and the sheriff sat beside him. There was a scattering of townspeople in the courtroom. They stared at Chris and Matt curiously. Doc pulled out his massive gold watch and looked at it. He cleared his throat. "I guess we'd just as well get on with it. Matt, suppose you start things off."

Matt rose and went to the witness chair. Sherm Logan brought the book and Matt put his hand on it. Sherm swore him in rapidly.

Doc Place looked at Matt. "Go ahead, Matt. Just tell us what happened in your own words."

Matt said, "I was asleep in the bunkhouse. A scream woke me up. I got up and ran into the house. I heard a second scream. Some of the men came in behind me and one of them lighted a lamp. Mrs. Knudson was lying at the bottom of the stairs. I went to her and covered her and then

86

I felt for a pulse but there wasn't one. She was dead."

Doc nodded. "Cause of death was a broken neck. She broke it in the fall." He waited a moment then said, "Go on, Matt."

"I went upstairs. Chris was in a daze but I got enough out of him to figure what happened."

"What did happen?"

Matt glanced apologetically at Chris, then angrily back at Doc. "We've been all over that. Why go into it again?"

"Have to, Matt. Go on. What happened?"

"Why Chris caught Wes with his wife. She panicked and ran out into the dark hallway. She fell down the stairs."

"What did Wes do?"

"He and Rudy Olguin got out of there as fast as they could."

"And what did you do?"

"I got Chris to sleep. Then I carried Mrs. Knudson upstairs. Then I saddled a horse and went after Wes."

"All right Matt. That's all."

Matt returned to his seat, relieved that he hadn't been required to lie under oath.

Doc called the crew members, one by one. The story they told was substantially the same as the one Matt had told. As they testified, Matt watched Chris's face. He did not seem to be listening to the testimony, but there was an expression of pain in his eyes. Matt could see he was oblivious to his surroundings and to the words being said in the courtroom. He was re-living that night with all its horror and shock and disillusionment. And he would go on re-living it.

Matt suddenly hated Wes more than he ever had before. He promised himself that he would kill Wes before he would let him hurt Chris this way again. Because if Chris didn't get some peace he was going to die.

Maybe that was what Wes was after. If Chris died Wes would inherit Fortress Ranch.

The testimony droned on. Neither Wes nor Olguin showed up to testify and Matt wondered whether they had ignored the coroner's summons or if Doc hadn't bothered to subpoena them.

At last Doc said, "All right, I guess that's all. From the testimony presented, it appears that Mrs. Knudson met her death accidentally from falling down the stairs. The inquest is adjourned."

Matt had to touch Chris's arm to get him to rise. He followed him out into the bright sunlight. Chris turned and looked at him. "You knew, didn't you Matt?"

"Knew what?"

"That Odie and Wes—well, that night wasn't the first time."

Matt wanted to lie. But Chris's eyes were so steadily on him that he couldn't bring himself to do it. He nodded reluctantly.

"When did it start?"

"Before Wes came home. I caught them together outside of town one day. I threatened Wes. I guess he figured if he came back—well, you'd be so happy about it that I'd keep still. And I did. When you told me he was back—when I saw your face—hell, Chris, I couldn't say anything."

Odie's funeral was brief. John Wilcox, the Methodist minister, gave a short sermon at the church and said a few solemn words at the graveside on the hill. No one was in attendance but Matt and Chris and the punchers from Fortress Ranch.

Afterward, Matt drove the buggy home. He hoped it was over. He hoped that now, at last, Wes would go away and let Chris forget the things he had done to him.

But some uneasy feeling in his chest told him Wes would never do that. Wes wanted Fortress and, one way or another, he would keep trying until either he or Chris was dead. The fact that Chris was Wes's father wasn't going to stop him from trying to kill him any more than it had stopped him from taking his father's wife under his father's roof.

It was going to be up to Matt to see that he didn't get away with it.

CHAPTER 9

Standing there in the inky yard at Fortress Ranch, Matt suddenly realized that the rain had stopped. An eerie stillness lay across the land, a stillness broken only by the soft drip of rainwater from the trees, by the distant and seemingly almost imagined roar of the river in the valley far below. No breeze stirred the air.

His premonition that Wes would continue trying to destroy old Chris had not been false, even though so far he had made no open and direct attempt on Chris's life. Obviously Wes realized that he could not inherit Fortress if he was convicted of killing Chris.

Perhaps he was hoping that Chris would be along when Fortress rode into Outlaw Canyon after the five hundred head of cattle he and the Taskers had stolen so brazenly a few days ago after a false report of rustling somewhere else had drawn Matt and the crew away. But he was in for a disappointment. Matt had no intention of letting Chris go along. He wasn't going to make it easy for Wes to kill him and escape the blame for it. Besides, Chris wasn't strong enough for such a ride.

Matt turned his head, listening. He thought he heard something, some distant sound. It was not repeated and he relaxed again. He reached automatically for tobacco and papers and made himself a smoke. He wiped a match alight on the seat of his pants and lighted it.

He turned his head again. This time he heard the sounds plainly in the stillness of the night—the suck of hoofs in the clinging mud, the scraping of a horse's passage through the wet brush beyond the yard.

He dropped his cigarette and put his foot on it. He glanced around to make sure he was not between the intruder and the lights of the house. Then he waited, strangely tense, but ready too.

The sounds grew as the intruder came closer. The possibility that the noise was being made by a loose horse occurred to him and he promptly discarded it. The horse was coming too fast for that.

He saw the dark shape of a horse dimly as it thundered into the yard and drew to a sliding, plunging halt before the back door of the house. He saw the figure that flung from the horse and stumbled toward the door.

In the light it seemed . . . He called, "Josie!"

The figure turned. Matt crossed to her in a dozen swift strides.

She was soaked and bedraggled and covered with mud. The horse stood with heaving sides and hanging head. Matt caught her to him and instantly felt the violent trembling that shook her slight form. He said, "Good God! Come on inside!"

He opened the door and pulled her indoors. He helped her out of her soaked jacket, shook down the stove and added wood. He opened the damper, then turned to look at her.

Her flaming hair hung in soaked strands on both sides of her face. She was pale, drawn, almost gaunt, but her eyes were enormous and they clung to his face desperately.

He said, "Just a minute," and hurried from the room. He took the stairs two at a time, got a thick bathrobe upstairs and hurried back with it. He took it into the kitchen. "Get out of those wet clothes and put this on."

She nodded numbly. Matt left her and went into the front room. He got the bottle of whisky, waited a few moments to give her time to change, then returned with it. He poured a glass half full and handed it to her. "Drink this down."

She took the glass, holding it in both hands. She took a gulp, made a face, then resolutely drank the rest of it.

She looked smaller to him in the bulky robe than she ever had before. He got her a towel and she dried her hair. The stove was roaring now, throwing off a wall of heat. She huddled close to it, still shivering.

He wanted to hold her, to stop her violent trembling. Instead he pulled the coffee pot from the back of the stove, to the front where it would heat. He said, "Something's happened. What is it?"

"They've set a trap for you, Matt, and those five hundred cattle were only the bait. They won't even be there when you ride into the canyon tomorrow. They're going to be driven out at dawn."

Her chin began to quiver and tears welled from her eyes. Matt put out his arms and closed them tight around her. He held her slight figure against his chest until her trembling quieted.

She was like a frightened kitten in his arms, warm, soft, comforted and still at last. He looked down at her. "Josie—I should never have let you get away from me."

She shook her head as though unwilling to talk about that now. She said, "They'll let you get well into the canyon, Matt. When you don't find the cattle and try to leave—they'll bottle you up. They mean to kill you, Matt. Then, in the confusion, Rudy and Wes and one or two others are going to leave. They're coming here to Fortress and they're going to kill Chris. They'll set fire to this house and leave Chris's body to burn. Nobody will be able to prove that the fire wasn't accidental and that Chris wasn't burned in it."

Matt stiffened. It was as close to a foolproof plan as anybody could devise. He asked, "How're they figuring on hiding the tracks of the cattle they drive out of there?"

"They won't try. They figure you'll send two or

three men to check out the tracks and bring the others on into the canyon."

Matt whistled softly. If he hadn't been warned, it would have worked. He would have done exactly that. And with all the shooting that would be taking place, no one would ever know who had killed whom. The fire at Fortress . . . Wes and Rudy couldn't be convicted of that because they would claim they had been in the canyon all the time.

Matt asked, "Do they know you're gone? Do they know you've come here?"

She refused to look at him. "They know I'm gone but they think it's something else. They don't know I'm here."

"Where do they think you've gone?"

"Not now, Matt. I don't want to talk about it now."

"All right, Josie." He got a cup and poured it full of coffee, which was now steaming hot. He handed it to her. She put her back to the stove and sipped it.

He said, "I'll wake the crew."

"You're not going into the canyon? Not after what I've just told you?"

"Not when they expect us, Josie. We'll go in early, before they can drive the cattle out."

She started to protest, but he didn't wait. He went out and crossed the yard to the bunkhouse. He lighted a lamp, then yelled, "Get out of your bunks and get dressed. Get saddled and ready to go." He waited until the men were awake, then said, "We've changed the plan a little. They're expecting us after sun-up so we'll go in before it's light."

He returned to the house across the muddy yard. Josie still waited by the stove. He smiled at her. "Feel better?"

She nodded, her eyes clinging to his.

He said, "Coming here like this—it took a lot of courage."

She didn't reply. He got himself a cup and filled it with coffee from the pot. He asked, "What do your brothers expect to get out of all this? Looks like Wes is the only one that's going to come out on top."

Her mouth took on a bitter twist. "Then you don't know them, Matt. They don't like Wes any better than you do, but they want Fortress Ranch. They're tired of being outcasts in the community. They're tired of being looked down on. They think if they can get their hands on Fortress, all that is going to change."

"How do they think they're going to manage it?"

"They'll manage it all right. They'll get an interest out of Wes first by threatening to expose him for killing Chris. And once they get part of it, the rest will be easy for them."

Matt frowned. If he went into Outlaw Canyon

before dawn it would mean that he went in without the support of the sheriff. There was no time now to send to town for a warrant and a posse.

Going in before dawn would also mean that Chris would be left alone or virtually so because he didn't dare leave enough men for an adequate guard. Leaving men behind would practically insure their defeat because they would be too short-handed to fight the bunch inside the canyon.

He asked, "What if we don't go in at all? What if we just refuse to take the bait?"

"Then I suppose they'll come here. They're not going to give up once they've gone this far. They could say you had poisoned Chris against Wes. They could even say you were the one Chris caught with Odie and that you threw the blame on Wes. If you're dead and if Chris is too—well, who's to say they were wrong?"

"The crew. They saw me run in here."

She smiled at him wearily. "They'll have thought of that. They could say you ran out to the bunkhouse while Chris was struggling with Odie. That you ran back in just after she fell downstairs. It isn't impossible. I'm telling you, Matt. Nothing's going to stop them. They've made up their minds that they're going to have this ranch and you're all that stands in their way. You and Chris."

Matt frowned, appalled at the complexity and

outright daring of the plan. It was fantastic, but it might very well work. The fact that Wes actually was Chris's son would weigh heavily in the courts. His utter rottenness would seem unbelievable, particularly if it was not supported with proof.

"How did you find this out?" he asked gently.

She glanced up at him briefly, flushing, both pain and shame plainly visible in her eyes. She lowered her glance almost immediately, and her voice was scarcely audible. "I'm one of them Matt. I'm a Tasker myself."

"There's more to it than that. They haven't forgotten that business at the school. They haven't forgotten the way you saved my neck the time I rode into the canyon after Wes. They wouldn't risk spilling the plan to you and they wouldn't let you ride out unless—"

"Matt, don't ask me any more questions. Please."

He stared down at the top of her damp head. He felt pity for her and anger at her brothers, at Wes and Olguin, but he felt confusion too.

He was ashamed of the thought that crossed his mind. What if Josie herself were a part of the devious plan the Taskers and Wes had cooked up between them? What if Josie's part in it was to confuse him and just make him think he knew the Taskers' plans?

He felt her eyes resting steadily on him. She

said, "I know what you're thinking, Matt, but it isn't true. I've run away from them and I'm never going back. They may be my family but they've been outlaws too long. They don't even think like decent people any more."

He said, "I'm sorry, Josie. I had no cause to be thinking the things I was." He had apologized and he meant the apology. But he knew there was more to it than Josie was telling him. Something had to have happened to make her leave her family and the canyon that had been her home since the day of her birth. Something terrible had to have happened to make her forget her loyalty to them. It had to be something that they had done to her.

He felt his anger rising recklessly. He asked, "What did they do to you, Josie? What did they do to make you leave like this—to make you say you're never going back?"

"Don't ask me that Matt. Please don't ask me now."

"But it was something they did, wasn't it?"

She nodded wordlessly, refusing now to meet his eyes. Her face was burning and hot.

What,? he thought. For God's sake, what? Had one of her own brothers tried to . . . ? He shook his head confusedly. No. The Taskers were a strange and wild and lawless bunch. But such a thing would be unthinkable to them.

Matt suddenly turned and strode angrily across

the room. He banged out the door and into the chilly night.

There was noisy activity at both bunkhouse and corral. A bunch of loose horses came thundering into the corral from the pasture, being driven by two yelling men.

Olguin? Could it have been Olguin? Could he have gotten Josie alone with her brothers' consent?

He shook his head again, remembering how infuriated Wiley had been at the thought of Josie and he carrying on at the school after everyone else had gone. No. But if it wasn't that, what could it be?

He counted the men in the yard, counted up those missing in his mind. They would ride into Outlaw's Canyon with no more than sixteen men including himself. And he had to leave one behind, at least. He couldn't take the chance of leaving Chris and Josie all alone.

Not that one man would do much good, if Wes and Olguin and a couple of others managed to get back here . . .

Tate Johnson, one of the hands, yelled at him, "How soon are we leavin', Matt?"

He shouted, "Pretty soon. Get your slickers and chaps. The brush is going to be wet. I'll be back in a minute and go over the plans with you."

He turned and hurried back across the yard to the house. Josie was sitting at the table, an empty coffee cup in front of her, staring emptily at the far wall. Matt went to her and put his hands on her shoulders. He asked, "Will you promise to stay here with Chris? You won't go running away again, will you?"

She glanced around and up. "I don't know where I'd go. Yes, I'll stay until you get back."

"Good. I'll leave one man. And there are lots of Odie's clothes upstairs if you'd like to put on something dry. Why don't you try and get some sleep?"

She smiled faintly. "Sleep, when I know where you're going?"

His hands tightened slightly. "I'll be back before we leave."

She nodded. He wondered briefly if she really would be here when he returned. She had a way of coming into his life only to step out of it again. But this time . . .

He released her shoulders, turned and went out the door.

CHAPTER 10

Josie heard the door slam. She heard Matt's heavy tread on the board floor of the porch. Terror for his safety touched her, but coupled with it was the deepest and bitterest kind of disillusionment. She supposed she deserved what Olguin had done to her, or tried to do, but for Wiley, her own brother, to permit it. . . .

She got up, biting her lower lip. She poured another cup of coffee and returned to the table with it. She sipped it, not caring that it scalded her mouth.

Ever since that first day in the schoolhouse near the mouth of Outlaw's Canyon she had wanted Matt. She had felt sorry for him at first and had been furious every time he was embarrassed by his lack of learning. But there hadn't been anything she could do about it until she got the idea of helping him.

It had been many days before she got up enough courage to stop him on his way home from school. She had been afraid that he would not accept her offer, and even more afraid that he would.

There had begun for her, then, a period of extreme happiness. She was with him every afternoon. She was alone with him and could watch his face as he pored over the books they studied, as he wrote with laborious attention to each word.

But it had been too wonderful to last. Wes's jealousy of Matt had seen to that. He'd gone to her brother Wiley with the lying story that she and Matt were "carrying on" at the school.

She hadn't known that Wiley had waylaid Matt until he got home that night. There was blood all over the front of Wiley's shirt and on his face. Every time he moved, his face twisted with pain.

Josie was in the kitchen helping her mother with the dishes when he came in. He crossed the room to her, whirled her around and slapped her savagely on the cheek so hard that her neck cracked. He said furiously, "Bitch! You damned little bitch, you're as bad as your ma!"

Josie glanced at her mother and saw that her face was pale. For an instant there was a spark of something in her mother's eyes. She licked her lips and started to speak. Then the spark was gone and she turned back to her dishes. Josie put a hand to her burning cheek, her eyes blank and uncomprehending.

Wiley slapped her again. "An' with that dirty stray from Fortress too!"

Josie was holding a plate. She threw it at him.

The plate struck him squarely in the face and shattered. Sharp edges cut him on the forehead and on one cheek. Blood welled from the cuts and he swiped at it automatically with the back of his hand. He stared at her in dumb surprise. Then his face turned dark with rage. "I'll show you, by

God! I'll beat some decency into you the way pa beat it into her!"

He unbuckled his gunbelt and slung it into a corner. He unbuckled his other belt and yanked it off. Doubling it in his right hand, he lunged toward her.

She tried to duck. She never knew whether he intended it or not, but his left hand caught the collar of her dress from behind. It tore as he yanked on it and the jerk brought her to her knees. His hand seized her underclothes and ripped them from the upper part of her body. Then the belt began to fall upon her naked back.

Even now she felt hot as she thought about it. The same welts seemed to burn across her back. She seemed to hear Wiley's harsh, ragged breathing, the obscenities and curses that poured from her mouth. She heard her mother's protesting, "Wiley! Stop!" but it was a halfhearted protest from a woman too terrified of her own off-spring to interfere.

Josie crawled under the table to get away. Beyond it, she got to her feet. She darted first one way and then the other, trying by her nimbleness to escape and get out the door.

She made it and ran past Wiley, but her dress, ripped from her shoulders, slipped down and tangled in her feet. She sprawled headlong.

Wiley yanked her up. His fist smashed into her face.

Now she realized that it was more than his belief that she had done something wrong that caused such uncontrollable rage in him. It was something twisted in Wiley himself, something connected with her mother and therefore with Wiley's attitude toward all women including Josie herself.

Court and Floyd, coming into the kitchen from the yard, stopped Wiley at last. And Josie fled from the room, to her own room where she stared into the mirror at her swelling eye, at her bruised and swollen mouth.

She dressed, but covering herself did not stop the feeling of being soiled. She'd done nothing wrong, but Wiley had soiled her beyond anything she could have done with Matt. She hated Wiley, and this canyon, and the house they lived in, and the way they lived.

What had Wiley meant when he said she was as bad as her ma? And why had he been so violent? Could it be possible that her mother . . . that . . . that she herself was not a Tasker at all? She felt stunned. It was the only explanation that could justify Wiley's bitter words. Her mother, overcome by the harshness of her life, her husband and sons, must have sought the softness she was missing with one of the transient "guests." Josie had been the result.

Obviously Ben Tasker had found out, for Wiley had said something about him beating her. And Wiley also knew.

Josie felt no bitterness toward her mother after the initial shock had passed. Only pity, and compassion, and a great relief to know that she was, perhaps, not a Tasker after all.

Anyway, who did Wiley think he was, condemning either her mother or herself for wrongdoing? Every one of her brothers, and Ben Tasker too, was a thief and probably a killer as well. Fortress cows and bulls had been the beginning of the Tasker cattle herd. Even now, they stole beef to eat rather than butcher their own. What gave them the right to blame either her mother or herself for rebelling against the medieval life they were forced to live in this God-forsaken place?

Outlaw Canyon was a rarity in nature, but ideal for the Taskers' purpose. From the canyon mouth to the rims that walled it on the north, it was a full twenty miles. In width, it varied from a mile to about five.

Far at the northern end, a creek cascaded off the rim in a waterfall several hundred feet high, and grew as it wound crookedly along the canyon floor until, at the canyon mouth, it became a fair-sized stream. The stream provided stock an irrigating water for the hay meadows, and water for domestic use.

There was only one entrance to this natural pocket, that at the canyon mouth. And it was narrow, guarded on both sides by steep piles of rock upon which nothing grew and which a horse could never climb.

Josie didn't know when the canyon had earned its name. It had been called Outlaw Canyon for as long as she could recall. But there had always been strangers in the canyon—cold, hard-eyed, rough-looking men who invariably went armed and who never stepped out the bunkhouse door but what their eyes scanned the surrounding countryside. Her father—in her mind she amended that—Ben Tasker had once told her they were hired hands, but they never worked. They just idled around the bunkhouse, playing cards and sometimes fighting among themselves in front of it. Once she had seen a man killed right in front of the bunkhouse door.

As she had grown, she had begun to reason things out a bit. For one thing, her father never paid his "hired hands." They paid him instead. The payments ranged from twenty-five dollars a month to more than a hundred depending, probably, on their ability to pay. When she asked Ben Tasker about this he became angry, but finally told her they were paying for their keep.

Her father, the one who had offered her mother the gentleness she must have hungered for, had probably been one of these. An outlaw himself, probably, or perhaps only a man who had, through no real fault of his own, gotten into trouble with the law. Josie wondered if he had been killed when Ben Tasker found him out. It was probable, she knew, but she didn't know whether to hate Ben for having killed him or to hate her real father for having made so much trouble for her mother. She suddenly felt thoroughly unhappy and confused. For her own peace of mind, she would have to stop guessing and assuming this and that. The thing for her to do was to go to her mother and ask her for the truth. She would, she promised herself, the first chance she got.

The transients came and went all through the years. Some stayed a couple of weeks and went on. Some stayed for months. And sometimes Ben Tasker and her brothers rode out of the canyon with several of these "guests," to be gone for days or even weeks. Once, Court came back with a bullet in his chest and from his delirious talk as she cared for him, Josie gathered that they had robbed a train.

He healed, eventually, and Josie never mentioned the things he had said in his delirium. But she made a resolve. She would leave the canyon when she was old enough. She would run away before she stopped caring that her brothers were thieves and murderers, before she became like her mother, afraid to open her mouth in protest against the things they did.

The things she had guessed about her true heritage lay silent in her heart through the passing months. Many times she almost asked her mother to tell her the truth, but each time she remained silent. She could not bear to add more pain to that already present in her mother's eyes. She could not bear to add more hurts to those her mother had already suffered. When she was fifteen, her mother died, and then it was too late to ask her for the truth.

It had been coming on for more than a year but, because the Tasker men never noticed Mrs. Tasker except when she didn't get their meals on time, they never knew that she was sick or that she was steadily growing worse. Josie knew it, though. And one day she rode into town herself to get Doc Place.

There was a terrible scene when she returned with him. Outsiders weren't welcome in the canyon, her brothers said.

They wouldn't let him near the house. They threatened to kill him if he tried to force his way inside. Josie and Doc were helpless in the face of the threats, which both knew were not idle ones. So Doc went back to town without seeing Mrs. Tasker, and a month later, Josie's mother died.

The funeral was a rough, homemade affair like the rough pine box they buried her in. The grave plot was out back of the house about three hundred yards. It contained the graves of three babies who had died before they were a year old, all of which had been carefully tended through the years by Mrs. Tasker and later by Josie herself.

Ben Tasker, and Josie, and Court and Wiley walked up the low hill in early morning behind the wagon containing the casket. Floyd drove. The grave had been dug the night before and they put the casket down into it and stood uneasily there, none of them knowing what to say.

Josie opened a Bible she had brought with her and read from it. She tried not to hate Ben Tasker and her brothers as she read. She tried not to remember that they had refused to let Doc Place into the house when he might have saved her mother's life. She tried to forget the years of toil and unhappiness that had brought her mother to this untimely end. But she could not help thinking that, even before her own birth, things must have been unbearable for her mother to have made her forget her marriage vows. And since then, it must have been much worse because neither Ben nor Wiley had ever forgiven her for the mistake Josie was now convinced she had made.

She read slowly and reverently from the Bible in her hands. Once Wiley broke in, "Get it over with, Josie, for Christ's sake!"

She looked at him with blazing eyes. "This is your mother, Wiley."

And old Ben said, "Shut up, Wiley, and let Josie do this the way she wants."

Afterward, with obvious relief, they filed back

down the hill while Court stayed to fill in the grave. Josie could still hear the rocks and clods hitting the thin pine box.

There was no break in the regular routine of canyon life. Josie just took up where her mother had left off. She kept the house and she cooked the meals. She washed clothes, and when she finished, she began all over again.

Josie was small, but she wasn't weak. Even so, she learned what it was to be tired when she got up in the morning, tired throughout the day and tired when she went to bed. And her resolve to leave whenever it was possible strengthened with the passing months.

After she passed sixteen, the year following her mother's death, she began to mature. Her body filled out. And the men who paraded in and out of the canyon began to notice her.

One in particular—a young, black-haired man with the same wary look to him all the others had. She didn't notice him at first. But she had the feeling, every time she went to the creek for water or into the yard to hang up clothes, that someone was watching her.

His name was Cling. Johnny Cling. She noticed him when he became more bold, lounging against the bunkhouse wall and frankly appraising her, though always when none of her brothers or her father were around.

She baked dried-apple pies one day and the

aroma of them cooling on the porch brought him to the door.

It was the closest look she had gotten of him and she didn't like what she saw. His eyes kept running up and down her body like a hand. His mouth, full-lipped, had an odd twist to it as though he were perpetually smiling, but no smile was in his eyes. "Those pies smell mighty good, girlie. Gonna give old Johnny Cling a piece?"

She said shortly, "Get out of here. You shift for yourself in the bunkhouse just like all the others do."

"If them pies are as sour as you, maybe I don't want a piece."

"Good. You wouldn't get one anyway."

He went to the edge of the porch and looked around. He turned and came back to her. "What you need is a little sweetenin'. And old Johnny Cling is an expert at sweetenin' girls."

"Is that where you got those claw marks on your face?"

Blood darkened his face and made the faint scars more noticeable. There was suddenly a wildness in his eyes that had not been there before. He had forgotten her father and brothers now. He had forgotten what the consequences of this might be.

Josie put the table between them. She said furiously, "You get out of here! They'll kill—"

He dived across the table, his hands clutching for her. She ducked but she was too late. The table overturned and both she and Cling tumbled to the floor. His hands ripped at her clothes. He began to chuckle softly, almost to himself.

Josie was wiry and strong, but she was no match for him. She clawed and bit and kicked, but it did no good. She felt smothered, suffocated. And then she heard heavy footsteps on the porch.

Apparently Cling heard them too, for he yanked his head around. He tried to scramble to his feet and his hand grabbed for the gun hanging from his side.

The roar of Wiley's rifle was deafening in the enclosed space. Cling was driven back against Josie, knocking her sprawling again. She fought clear and got to her feet. There was a large stain of blood on the palm of one of her hands. She wiped it dazedly on what was left of her skirt.

Wiley looked at her wildly. He choked, "You God damned Jezebel, you're exactly like her now. There's blood on your hands just like there was on hers!" And he turned and walked outside.

CHAPTER 11

Wiley avoided her as much as possible after that and she was just as glad, but it was hard for her to forget what had happened in the kitchen. It was hard for her to forget her terror and desperation as she fought with Cling, and difficult to forget her horror at his death.

Life continued much as usual in the canyon. Josie kept house and cooked and washed. The Tasker men continued to run their little business of harboring outlaws. They had obviously served notice to their "guests" that she was to be let alone after the incident with Cling, because the "guests" avoided her scrupulously.

She began to see Wes Knudson occasionally in the canyon. And one day Wes drove a small bunch of Fortress cattle into the canyon and sold them to Wiley for ten dollars a head.

He appeared in the canyon more frequently after that, and occasionally ate supper with them. Several times a month he brought in a bunch of cattle which he sold to Wiley for considerably less than the going price.

The drudgery and monotony of her work, coupled with the total lack of appreciation, gradually drove her to leave the house whenever she could get away. She would saddle up a horse and ride to the upper end of the canyon where she would dismount and lie on the grass and stare up at the waterfall. There was beauty in the world. The evidence of it was here in this waterfall. There was love, not the kind Cling had tried to force on her but another kind, a decent, generous kind of love.

She knew she would never find it here. Inside Outlaw Canyon there was nothing but greed and ugliness. And sometimes death.

Soon, very soon, she would be old enough to leave. But she must plan her escape very carefully, else Ben and her brothers would come after her and bring her back.

She began riding to the mouth of the canyon as well as to its upper end and there was purpose in her doing so. She wanted them to become used to seeing her ride that way so that when she left they would not immediately suspect that she had run away. . . .

Sitting here in the kitchen at Fortress, dressed only in the voluminous, heavy robe Matt had given her, she remembered it all.

A day like any other day, she remembered. She had finished her morning's work and had saddled up for a ride. She had headed toward the canyon's mouth, thinking of the time when she would ride this way for the last time, of the day she would ride away, never to return.

Gunshots from the direction of the canyon mouth startled her. Then, a few minutes later, her brothers thundered past her heading toward the shots.

Apparently they had also heard. Sensitive to the danger they always faced from the law outside this place, they were hurrying to investigate.

There were more gunshots. Out of curiosity, Josie spurred her horse.

The first thing she saw was a small bunch of cattle standing in the road. Her practiced eye instantly read their brands.

Fortress cattle. Another bunch that Wes was bringing in. But someone had followed Wes, stopped him, and that explained the gunfire she had heard.

Fear suddenly touched her heart. Who, on Fortress, would stop the boss's son and exchange shots with him? Only one man would dare do that. Matt Springer. And if it was Matt, he was pinned down, with Wes and her three brothers against him. Against that kind of odds, he didn't have a chance.

Josie didn't hesitate. Her spurs raked her horse's sides. The animal sprang ahead and thundered down the road.

She saw the man she believed was Matt almost at once but he was pinned down behind a rock and she couldn't see his face. Across the creek, she could see Wes Knudson as he turned to stare at her. She saw her three brothers, ducking from rock to rock as they tried to flank the intruder's position.

The shooting stopped as she pounded into the middle of it. Floyd yelled angrily, "Josie! Damn it, get out of here before you get shot!"

Her head pounding furiously, she called, "Matt? Are you all right?"

She held her breath, waiting for his reply.

Relief made her weak when she saw him get up and sprint toward her. Her heart stopped for fear one of her brothers, or Wes, would shoot him while he was exposed. Then she realized they were holding their fire for fear of hitting her.

Matt reached her, sweating heavily. His face was covered with dust. She said, "Get up behind me. They won't shoot because they'll be afraid of hitting me."

He leaped up behind her and she dug her spurs in frantically. Her horse, bearing its double burden, thundered down the road and around a bend.

It seemed as though she had been holding her breath forever. She felt dizzy and weak. She vaguely remembered asking him if he had been hit and seemed to remember him saying something about her saving his life. But her impressions weren't clear. Her heart beat rapidly within her chest. The dizziness and light-headedness did not go away.

They reached the canyon mouth and she headed the horse directly for the river. They splashed into it and almost immediately the horse began to swim. Matt slipped out of the saddle and let the horse tow him along. She found herself wishing he would take her away with him, that they could ride on and on, away from Outlaw Canyon, away from Fortress, to a new life where there were no Taskers and no Wes Knudsons, but only the two of them. Like in the fairy stories she'd read as a child in school.

Then her practical side took hold. She was an empty-headed girl and not pretty enough to be wanted by someone like Matt. No. She'd take him far enough toward Fortress so that he'd be safe. Then she'd turn and ride back to the weather-beaten house in Outlaw Canyon, to Ben Tasker and her brothers, to their endless parade of "guests."

Unless . . . unless she *made* Matt want her so badly that he'd never let her go.

They talked some as they rode, but she couldn't remember what they said. All she remembered was the sharp, almost painful pleasure of being close to him. All she remembered was her own fear, her shame at what she intended to do. And her implacable determination to do it anyway.

The sun was a blazing flame in the west. The horse, carrying his double load, labored up the slope beyond the river through high, fragrant brush, until he reached the even more fragrant pines above. Here Josie stopped the heaving horse to rest and Matt slipped from his back to the ground.

The tension in Josie was intolerable. The ridge was in shadow and Matt was shivering from the cold in his wet clothes. She felt an immediate compassion for him. She dismounted and untied her blanket roll from the saddle. She handed him a blanket and he took off his shirt and put it over his shoulders. She started to spread the other one on the ground, but he took it from her and spread it himself. He sat down on it.

Her face feeling uncomfortably hot, Josie sat down beside him and began to pull off her wet boots. Did he understand what was in her mind? Did he know that she meant to trap him into caring for her?

The boots would not come off, so Matt helped her with them. And before he was through, they both were laughing. . . .

Why had it ended the way it had? Was it her fault, or his? She remembered how he had stopped laughing and flung himself down on the blanket beside her.

And then she had been in his arms, his mouth eager against hers. She hadn't been able to think, or speak. She had been his and he had been hers and she hadn't had to trap him after all.

It was like flying, and then falling, and at last it was a little like dying. But when it was over, Josie's mind began to work again and she felt a deep, overpowering shame because if she hadn't trapped him she had wanted and planned to do so and must therefore pay the penalty for it.

How could a man love a woman who gave herself so freely to him? How could he help but wonder how many others had come before him in her arms? And how many would come after him?

Her own guilt prompted her after that. When he said he was sorry she twisted his words around until they seemed to mean something entirely different from what she knew they meant. Angry and ashamed, she ran away from him, giving him no opportunity to explain.

Why? Why had she been such a fool? He had wanted her that night and would have taken her away with him. Yet she knew that forever afterward she would have wondered if it was because he felt an obligation to do so or because he really loved her as he said he did. So she had thrown away her chance for love. She had thrown Matt away. She had ridden back into Outlaw Canyon to take up her life where she had left off earlier that day. Like something whipped and cowed. Like something beaten and without hope. Like her mother in that hour of returning home.

Back to her three brothers and aging Ben Tasker. Back to their hard, condemning eyes and their ugly, angry words. They weren't worried that Matt would bring either the sheriff or the Fortress crew.

They knew Chris Knudson and they knew Matt. Neither would lodge a complaint against Wes over five steers. Nor would Fortress come by itself, particularly since it had been Wes, not the Taskers, who had stolen the steers.

But they were furious with Josie. Wiley would have whipped her with his quirt but Court stopped him, saying, "What the hell's the matter with you, anyway? She may be a tramp but she's your sister and you ain't no better anyway. You'll bed with anything that'll have you and you don't give a damn where you do it, either. So why be high an' mighty with her?"

Wiley looked poisonously at her. "That damned Cling first. Now Matt. She's worse'n ma."

Josie cringed. To have Wiley compare Cling's attack on her to what she and Matt had shared. . . . Tears welled in her eyes. Her mouth trembled in spite of her determination to hold it firm.

She ran from the room, but she could hear them arguing, cursing, shouting, long after she had left.

Josie herself could have taken the initiative after that. She could have slipped out of the canyon and gone to see Matt. She could have insisted that her brothers let her go to town sometimes when they went in for supplies. And maybe she would have seen Matt there.

But she hadn't gone. She hadn't known . . . hadn't been sure that he wanted her. She felt instinctively that if he did want her, not even the

120

peril of entering Outlaw Canyon would have stopped him from coming after her.

And he hadn't come, thus strengthening her belief that he didn't want her for his wife.

Suddenly she beat her fists against the table top. She knew now that she had been wrong. Matt had wanted her all right. He hadn't come after her because he'd thought she didn't want him to.

She got up and went to the door. She stared out into the yard. There was much activity there, men milling around, horses pitching as they were mounted and raked with the spurs. They'd be leaving soon.

She wondered what was going to happen to them. Would Matt be killed? Her heart felt as though a cold hand had closed over it.

Some of the members of her own family would certainly be killed. And she would be responsible. But she didn't regret coming to warn Matt. She'd do exactly the same thing again.

She returned to the table and sat down wearily. The long, wet ride, the chilling, the tension she'd been under were beginning to tell on her. But her mind and her memory would not let her rest.

It had been impossible to live in the Tasker house without knowing when something was going on. Even if the men living there were careful with their talk as they were after she had saved Matt from them.

She would catch a word here, a fragment of a sentence there. It had been a long time before the fragments made sense to her. But when they did. . . .

First of all, they hated Wes and held him in contempt. That, perhaps, had been the first thing that had made her realize something was in the wind. If they hated him, why did they let him spend so much time inside the canyon? Why did they do business with him?

The intent came first. They made up their minds that somehow, through Wes, they could steal Fortress Ranch. Once the idea was in their minds all that remained was to work out the details.

She found herself thinking of Wes. What had happened to make him hate Matt so? Why did he hate his father enough to kill him now?

It was jealousy, she supposed. Jealousy of Matt and resentment toward his father because his mother had, consciously or unconsciously, pitted them against each other from the very start.

Chris's bringing Matt home had only intensified the feelings of resentment that were already present in Wes.

The terrible part of it all was that Fortress belonged to Wes. He didn't have to steal it. All he had to do was go home and tell Chris he was sorry. All he had to do was prove to the old man that he had changed. Chris would like nothing better than to be able to believe it.

But getting the ranch that way wouldn't satisfy Wes's hate. He wanted to see his father dead and he wanted Matt dead too.

Josie shook her head. Something was wrong with Wes, something that only death could cure.

CHAPTER 12

Josie realized now that her brothers had deliberately planned the episode that had resulted in Odie's death.

She hadn't paid much attention at first. There was always a lot of talk going around inside Outlaw Canyon. That was inevitable in a virtually womanless community. But this talk had an edge to it.

They ribbed Wes about having left home too soon. They talked about Odie and went into considerable detail describing her visible charms and speculating about her invisible ones.

But when they started hinting that Matt Springer was probably keeping Odie satisfied at Fortress, they got under Wes Knudson's skin. The ribbing became more pointed and at last Wes took the bait. He got acquainted with Odie in town and it wasn't long before she was meeting him a couple of times a week.

If Matt hadn't discovered them, Josie had no doubt her brothers would have seen to it that both Matt and Chris found out what was going on. Because they already had a plan, one that included Matt's and Chris's death.

Only it didn't work out exactly that way. Wes was infatuated with Odie. He figured the only way to keep seeing her was to move back to Fortress Ranch.

He waited until Matt went away for several days. Then, taking Rudy Olguin with him, he returned to Fortress and made his peace with Chris.

Chris, disillusioned and heartbroken, was only too glad to believe Wes's lies. So Wes and Rudy moved in at Fortress. And events continued to march toward tragedy.

Josie had never really liked Olguin, but that wasn't surprising because she never liked any of the men who came to Outlaw Canyon, stayed briefly and went away.

Decent men didn't come. Only men wanting to hide out from the law until the hue and cry died down.

Olguin was one of these. She didn't know how many men he had killed, but one of them, shot in a saloon brawl in Sante Fe, happened to have brothers who cared about what happened to him.

With half a dozen of their friends, they took Olguin's trail. And when he realized how implacably they were following him, he came to the canyon for refuge, to wait until they gave up the search.

Olguin was about thirty, she supposed. Though short, he was taller than Josie by about an inch. He was only barely conscious when he rode in after Odie's death, escorted by Wiley and Court who had ridden to the canyon mouth to investigate the shots.

They brought him into the house and laid him on the lumpy sofa in the living room. They called Josie and she cut away the bloodsoaked shirt to expose the wound.

The bullet had struck his upper arm, breaking the bone but not shattering it. The bullet had flattened, though, and the damage to the flesh of his arm was terrible. He fainted from loss of blood as they carried him inside.

She had them carry him upstairs and she poured whisky liberally over his wound. She bandaged it and, with her brothers' help, managed to splint the arm. She wanted them to fetch Doc Place, but they refused.

She could only guess why they wanted to save Olguin. He would hate savagely the man who had wounded him. Hating, he would be useful to the Taskers in carrying out their plan.

Caring for Olguin meant, temporarily at least, that she gave up her horseback rides. She was up and down the stairs a hundred times a day. Whenever she could spare time out from cooking and washing and keeping house, she went up and sat with him.

He was a human being, whatever else he might be, and he was in pain. Josie did all she could to ease his pain and make him comfortable, but beyond that there was little she could do. She could only wait.

For two days he lay unconscious, as though in a

coma, not moving, just breathing harshly and unevenly. On the third day, his face was red and hot with fever and she knew the wound had infection in it.

She got Court and Floyd to hold him and she took the bandage from his upper arm. It was festering. She said, "Look at it. Now will you get Doc Place? He's going to die if you don't, and he'll lose the arm even if you do."

"It's his left," Floyd said unfeelingly.

"Then I'll go for Doc."

Court shook his head. "Pa wouldn't let you get Doc Place for ma. What makes you think he'll let you get him for Rudy?"

"But—"

"You just watch him and take care of him. Not your doin' if he dies."

Josie shrugged, cleaned and re-bandaged the wound. She and Court re-set the splint. She knew how useless it would be to ride in after Doc Place. Even if he would come, there wasn't a chance of getting him into the canyon and into the house. Not against opposition from Ben Tasker and her three brothers.

Later that day, Olguin began to mutter with delirium. She would catch some snatches of his talk that made sense but most times it would seem to be just words.

Wes came in to see him that afternoon. Both of his eyes were black. His mouth was still cracked and puffy after three days. He limped noticeably.

Josie watched him as he stood looking down at Olguin. She said, "You've seen him. Now get out of here. He's talked enough since he's been delirious so that I know what you two have done."

Wes turned his head. "That damned Matt did this to us."

"You had it coming and more. I wish—"

"What do you wish?" His face was ugly and his eyes were cold.

"I wish he'd killed you both."

He left the bedside and took a couple of steps toward her. She laughed humorlessly. "I wouldn't if I were you. My brothers aren't much but they're death on anyone who touches me."

He stopped. Josie said, "Get out of here and don't come back. If he dies I'll let you help bury him."

She was ashamed of herself after Wes had left. She was getting to be just as callous and cold as the rest of the Taskers. Life was losing its value. She had seen too much of death.

And because she was ashamed, she spent more time with Olguin. And slowly he began to heal until, three weeks after he had been shot, he was able to sit up a little while each day in bed.

In his weakness, Olguin exhibited an agreeable helplessness never apparent in him when he was well. He showed dependence on Josie and, because of her own deep loneliness, she began to enjoy her talks with him.

He probably told her more of his past then he had ever told a living soul. He told her of his father and of the beatings his father gave both his mother and himself—until the day he shot his father, dragged him out and buried him, then ran away from home.

Sometimes he talked big but there were moments when she knew his words were true. He confessed to being terrified after leaving home. He got a job as choreboy on a ranch in Kansas. He received the usual, thorough riding from the crew.

He understood now, he said, that the riding had been good natured and harmless. But he hadn't understood that then. And he'd shot one of his tormentors in the back.

They hauled him, skinny and dirty and scared, to Dodge City and put him in jail. Because of his age, he was released into the custody of a livery stable operator and his wife while he awaited trial. He ran away from them, stole a horse and rode west. He eluded the pursuit and this fact still puzzled him.

There began after that one of the most terrible of ordeals, one that still gave him nightmares. It was an ordeal of hunger and loneliness and thirst. And it was a miracle that he survived.

He ate insects and grass and sometimes roots. He was picked up, little more than skin and bones, by a wandering band of Arapaho, and adopted by a family that had lost their own son recently to disease.

He stayed with them almost a year, during which time he gained weight and grew. He learned to ride well and to shoot equally well. He learned to hunt and to butcher meat, skills that would be useful to him later on. He learned to trail where the average man would see no trail. And he learned to hide his own trail so well that no one but an Indian could follow it.

But killing punctuated this chapter of his life just as it had the other ones. He quarreled with another brave and killed again.

Josie, in conflict with herself, could not help but pity him because obviously he had never been given the chance to be anything but what he was. Killing his brutal father had apparently taught him that killing was, at least, an expedient solution to whatever problems were facing him. Given a different environment, she knew he might have been a completely different kind of man.

Spending as much time as she did with him, she knew when he began to think of her as more than just his nurse. And, feeling trapped and lonely, knowing Matt was lost to her, she could not help being pleased by it.

The thought crossed her mind that her brothers would probably accept it if she married Olguin, and then she angrily put the thought away from her. Marrying Olguin would be no escape but only a continuation of the same kind of life she had always led. And it would be a betrayal of what she felt for Matt.

Olguin's wound mended, but slowly, because of the infection that had poisoned it. The bone, inexpertly set, healed crookedly. He was bitter, and he hated Matt for being the cause of it. He swore he would kill Matt if it was the last thing he ever did.

Understanding the extent of his hatred for Matt, Josie was frightened. She briefly considered marrying Olguin next time he asked her and getting him to take her away without first revenging himself on Matt. But she knew it was hopeless. Olguin hated too well to give up his plans for Matt.

CHAPTER 13

Not long afterward, it became obvious to Josie that something was in the air. Olguin's arm was almost completely healed and though it hung crookedly at his side and plainly pained him when he used it, he began to spend less and less time with Josie and more in the company of her brothers.

He was with Wes more, too, and Wes was now inside the canyon more than he was out. Olguin made himself agreeable to Wes and this was puzzling because Josie knew Olguin detested Wes.

Why, she wondered. And the feeling of hidden crosscurrents flowing back and forth within the valley grew increasingly disturbing to her.

The weeks passed and, instead of decreasing, the feeling of tension within the canyon increased. It was similar to the tension everyone had been under in the past when they were planning some dangerous job outside the confines of the canyon.

And for some reason, with the increase of tension, Josie's fear and uneasiness grew. Several times she tried to get Court or Floyd to tell her what was going on. Each time they laughed at her for worrying and refused to talk.

There was only one person from whom she could find out. That was Olguin and the only way she would get him to talk was by making him think she was interested in him and was considering his proposal of marriage.

And so, whenever he was in the canyon, she went out of her way to be nice to him.

One evening in July, after fixing a supper she knew he liked, she stopped him as he was going out of the kitchen door. She pretended to be hurt. "You've been avoiding me. I thought you wanted to marry me."

He turned and grinned at her. "You mean you're ready?"

"I might be sooner if you'd spend more time with me. But all you want to do is hang around in town with my brothers and Wes."

"We haven't been going to town. Something's up, that's all, and it takes a lot of working out."

"What's up, that's as important as all that?"

"I can't tell you now. But I can tell you this much. When it's over and we're married you can have anything you want. Anything!"

"I suppose it's another train job or something. Last time they tried that, Court got shot. If you think I'm going to sit around wondering where you are and even if you're going to come back or not, you're mistaken."

"This isn't that kind of job. This one's foolproof and there's a hell of a lot more in it than in any train or bank job. You'll have to take my word for that."

"Why should I take your word for anything?"

"Don't be like that, Josie." He tried to come closer to her but she stayed out of his reach. "Play along and you can have anything you want. We can even take a trip, to New York or San Francisco or someplace."

"How do you expect to get the money for that?" she asked suspiciously. "Steal it?"

"We ain't going to steal nothing, Josie. Not right out anyway. We're just going to borrow something for a while."

"What are you talking about?"

"Never mind. You'll find out when it's time. I'll build you a house to live in and I'll have a share in a hundred thousand acres of land."

He put his arms around her and kissed her on the mouth. She turned her head and he started to pull away. Then he stared down at her. His eyes took on a strange glow, one that was frightening.

His hands suddenly became like claws, digging into her arms. His fingers were like steel.

She pushed violently against his chest. "You wait."

The kitchen door slammed open. Court said, "Yeah, Rudy. You wait, unless you want Wiley on your tail."

Olguin released her and both men went outside. Josie began to do the dishes, frowning worriedly. What had Olguin meant about a big house and all the money she wanted? What had he meant about an interest in a hundred thousand acres of land?

There wasn't but one place that big for more than a hundred miles. Fortress Ranch.

Could they be planning . . . ? She shook her head. It wasn't possible. And then she frowned. Why wasn't it? Wes was thick with Olguin and her brothers these days and Wes was Chris Knudson's heir. If Chris was dead. . . . But what had Rudy meant about borrowing something for a while?

She finished the dishes abstractedly. She thought of Matt and suddenly she felt like crying. All she wanted in the world was Matt, but she was a Tasker and all that was going to be available to her was Rudy Olguin. Well, she wasn't going to marry *him*. She'd make him think she was until she found out what she wanted to know. And if their plan *was* to take Fortress. . . .

Dejectedly she went up to bed. She didn't know how she could stop them even if they were planning some way of taking Fortress. But if she knew the details she could at least warn Matt.

She spent a sleepless night trying to make some sense out of Olguin's cryptic remarks. The plan, whatever it was, was almost ready to be put into operation. The tension, the sense of urgency apparent in her brothers, in Olguin, and particularly in Wes, had increased in the last day or two. That left her very little time.

In the morning, she put on her best dress. Today, she had decided, she would flirt with Olguin shamelessly. And perhaps by tonight she would know what was going on.

He lingered over his coffee until the others left, his gaze never leaving her. The same glow she had seen in his eyes before was in them today. Her own deliberately provocative attitude accounted for part of it. But she realized that part of it was something else.

He waited until he heard the others shouting out at the corral. Then he got up and came toward her.

"We're leavin' this morning, Josie."

She turned from the stove to face him. "Leaving for where?"

"Never mind. But it's the start of what I was tellin' you about. We can get married when I get back."

"*If* I agree."

He caught her in his arms. She started to struggle, then forced herself to stop. She raised her face and looked into his eyes. They were burning and they frightened her. He kissed her lingeringly.

She was sure, now, that she could never marry him. She said, "Maybe I won't even be here when you get back. If you won't even trust me enough to tell—"

He chuckled. "You're too nosy. Maybe I'll tell you when I get back." He released her and, grinning, went outside. She stood at the back door, watching, as her brothers, Olguin and Wes rode out.

She went upstairs and changed. She hadn't succeeded very well in finding out what she had to know. But perhaps when Olguin got back she could do better.

They were gone three days. The first sign of their return was a monstrous dust cloud rising into the air in the direction of the canyon mouth. She heard the sound, the low bawling of many cattle next. And then she saw the herd and walked out into the yard so that she could check the animals' brands as they rumbled ponderously past. Fortress cattle. And there must be five hundred of them.

They drove the cattle into a fenced pasture that nestled against the rim west of the house. They were jubilant when they came in. Wiley got a couple of bottles and they sat on the front porch, passing the bottles around. They all began to get a little drunk.

Listening, she heard Wiley say, "Well, that's the first step and it went off without a hitch. Matt Springer and his crew will be madder'n hell when they find out that drifter lied about seeing Fortress cattle being driven off the other side of the Mesa. And when they do get back and find five hundred head gone from there—oh, boy!"

What would Matt do, Josie asked herself. The answer was easy. He would round up a bunch of men and come after them.

None of it seemed to make much sense. Apparently they expected Matt to discover the loss, even wanted him to. They wanted him to come into the canyon after the stolen herd.

The light faded from the sky. Josie got supper on and called the men. Olguin was unsteady on his feet. After supper the others left and went to the bunkhouse for a poker game. But Olguin stayed.

Josie went to her room and got out the only bottle of perfume she owned. She applied it liberally. She brushed her hair carefully and went back downstairs. Olguin tried to catch her but she avoided him and ran out onto the front porch.

She stared up at the graying sky. Clouds were piled high on all sides, clouds that seemed to grow blacker with the fading light.

Olguin came out behind her and put his arms around her waist. She could feel his hands trembling. He said hoarsely, "Quit putting me off, Josie. I told you I'd give you any damn thing you want."

She turned her head and laughed provocatively. She twisted in his arms and put her own arms up around his neck. She pressed her body close to his.

His arms tightened savagely and for an instant panic touched her mind. She asked, "What if I said I would? Wouldn't you think, then, that I was entitled to know what was going on?"

He kissed her and she returned the kiss, though it was hard for her to do. When he broke away, breathing rapidly, she said, "Well, wouldn't you?"

"Sure. I guess I would."

"Well, I will marry you."

He kissed her again, his arms holding her so tightly she could scarcely breathe. She was playing with fire because there was violence in him now, violence that would not be denied. She spoke with her head turned and resting against his chest. "What did you mean about building me a house?"

"Fortress money is going to build that house." His voice was impatient, as though he thought she shouldn't be thinking of houses at a time like this.

"You mean money from the cattle you stole?"

"Those cattle are only bait. We're going to have the whole damned thing."

"How are you going to manage that?"

"Chris is going to burn to death in that big old house. And Wes will inherit the ranch. Only Wes will do exactly what he's told because if he don't he'll hang for killing Chris."

"What do you mean about the cattle being bait?"

"They won't be here tomorrow when Matt comes after them, that's all. We're going to drive them out at dawn. Which will make Matt's coming here look like an unprovoked attack. We'll bottle them up in here by stopping up the gorge. Then Wes and me and a couple of others will go to Fortress and burn the house and get rid of the old man."

Josie tried to pull away, without success. Olguin

muttered, "That's enough talk. You think I'm made of ice? I want you, damn it, and I'm going to have you—now!"

"We're not married yet." Her voice sounded small and scared.

"But you've promised to marry me. That's close enough."

She struggled. "My brothers—"

She heard Wiley laugh unexpectedly from the shadows beyond the porch. His voice, when he spoke, was thick with anger. "Your brothers won't do a goddam thing! I been watchin' the way you been teasin' him. Now, by God, you can pay the fiddler. None of us is goin' to interfere. Take her upstairs, Rudy. Take her upstairs an' do what you please with her."

She opened her mouth to scream for Floyd and Court, but Olguin clamped a hand over it. He dragged her in the door and toward the stairs.

She continued to struggle and he struck her savagely with his fist. Stunned, momentarily unable to struggle, she felt herself being carried up the stairs. Olguin might not be very big, but he was strong.

She was in her bedroom with him when her senses returned and he was tearing at her clothes.

She broke away and fell to the floor on the other side of the bed. Her hand touched a bootjack halfway under the bed.

She grasped it in both hands and when he came

after her, sprawled full length across the bed and reaching, she slammed it fiercely against the side of his head.

Stunned, he cursed her. She got to her knees and struck him again, still holding the wooden boot-jack in both hands.

He tried to roll and get away. She got up and struck him a third time, with every bit of strength she possessed.

Olguin collapsed, halfway on the bed, halfway off, and remained still. Josie stood there trembling for an instant. Then she ripped off what was left of her dress, snatched a skirt and blouse from the closet and tremblingly put them on. Near hysteria, she ran down the stairs and out into the night.

Court, coming toward the house from the bunkhouse, tried to stop her but she brushed past. She ran to the corral, with Court lumbering protestingly along behind. She untied a saddled horse that was tied to the corral fence and vaulted to the saddle. She thundered out of the yard.

Court would find out soon enough what had happened, from Wiley and from Olguin. They'd figure that was why she'd run away. They wouldn't realize she intended warning Matt and they'd be too busy tonight and tomorrow to think of coming after her.

She pounded toward the canyon mouth. And as she did, the wind began to rise and it started to rain.

CHAPTER 14

The ride to Fortress was a nightmare that Josie would not soon forget. Before she reached the canyon mouth, the wind had increased until it threatened to tear her clothes from her body with its force. And the rain came down in sheets and pelted against her with a force that made her face burn fiercely and at last turn numb.

Fortunately for Josie, she reached the river before it rose to flood stage, before it became filled with floating snags and debris. She swam her horse across, now soaked to the skin and chilled all the way to her bones.

Her teeth chattered and her body trembled violently. She clenched her jaws determinedly and kept on. Eventually she reached Fortress and Matt.

Now she got up and went to the kitchen door. She stared out into the yard at the preparations under way.

Most of the men had their horses caught and saddled, but two or three were still inside the corral, roping out horses from the milling bunch. She couldn't see Matt, so she turned away from the door.

She lighted another lamp, picked it up and headed up the stairs. She didn't know which had been Odie's room but she had no difficulty in finding it.

She found a riding skirt, a blouse and a small pair of boots and put them on. It made her feel strange to be wearing a dead woman's clothes, but she knew she should be practical. Her own clothes were not only wet; they were ruined. And she couldn't stay here in a man's bathrobe.

Dressed, she went back into the hall and headed for the stairs. Chris was just coming out of his room, fully dressed, carrying a lamp. His face was old and gaunt and tired, but there was determination in his eyes.

He smiled at her. "Hello Josie. What are you doing here?"

She answered with a question of her own. "And what are you doing up? You're supposed—"

"Damn what I'm supposed to do! I'm going with Matt."

She went downstairs, with Chris following her. Matt was standing beside the kitchen stove, a cup of coffee in his hand. His boots were covered with mud. He looked at Chris in surprise. "I thought you'd gone to bed."

"I got up. I'm going with you. This is my job and I'm going to do it or know the reason why. Just because Wes happens to be my son—"

Matt shook his head. "You're not going, Chris. I won't let you go. The river will be flooding and the bridges will all be out. We'll have to swim the horses across—"

"I've done it before."

143

"I know you have, and you'll do it again. But you can't stand it tonight and you know you can't."

"Who says I can't?"

"I do. Besides, Josie's going to be staying here. Somebody's got to look after her."

The old man stood there, balked and helpless. But there was also visible in his eyes the knowledge that what Matt had said was true.

Matt said, "That cattle herd was bait. They want us to come in there but they're expecting us after sun-up tomorrow. So we're going in while it's still dark and we'll give them a little surprise."

"That what Josie came to tell you?"

Matt nodded. He went over and slapped Chris lightly on the back. "We'll be back by noon."

"I don't feel right—"

"I don't know why the hell you shouldn't. The boss can't do everything. That's why he's got a crew."

He went out onto the porch and Josie followed him. He was thinking Chris ought to go to town or someplace where it was safe but he could never hurt Chris that way, sending him off to safety like a woman or a child. He started to speak, but Josie said, "Watch out for Olguin, Matt. He blames you because his arm is crooked. He blames you for all the pain. He's the most dangerous of the lot."

Matt ignored her warning. "When this is over, I want you with me, Josie. I want you to marry me."

Her glance was defenseless. "Yes Matt."

He caught her in his arms. For the first time in months she felt safe and warm. She whispered, "He was awful, Matt. He—"

He put a hand lightly to her mouth. "That why you left?"

She nodded. "And Wiley—Wiley even encouraged him. But it was partly my fault, I guess. I made him think—well, I had to know what they were planning, even if—"

"Don't talk about it," Matt said. "Don't even think about it. You got away and you don't ever have to go back."

Her arms were suddenly very strong, very fierce as they clung to him. A chill of fear traveled up her spine. With her face buried in his chest, she whispered fearfully, almost to herself, "Don't go, Matt. Please don't go. Something terrible is going to happen if you do."

Matt Springer looked down at Josie's smooth hair which had, so recently, been soaked and muddy too. He felt a vast tenderness for her, but he felt something else as well: hunger stronger than any he had ever felt before. He wanted tonight to be finished with. He wanted to be with Josie, every day and every night of his life to come.

Her life, until now, had been brutal and ugly, with neither love nor tenderness to temper its ugliness. Yet it hadn't hardened her. It hadn't dimmed the hope in her or killed the spark that made her what she was.

Not that it wouldn't, given time. Matt meant to see to it she did not go back.

He had a moment's concern, thinking that nothing was certain about tomorrow. Riding into Outlaw Canyon was a highly risky undertaking, even with the element of surprise on Fortress's side.

An invading force would necessarily be exposed on the canyon floor. Exposed to sharpshooters in the rocks on either side. For all Matt knew the Taskers had dynamite planted on the steep hillsides so that they could bottle up any invading force and wipe them out at their convenience.

And there was another thing. Even if Matt himself wasn't hurt or killed, Josie's brothers and father were among those who would be fighting him. It was practically a certainty that one or more of them would be hit. Could Josie forgive him if he killed the members of her family?

He said, "You know what may happen tomorrow, don't you? We're going to kill some of the members of your family. Maybe all of them. How are you going to feel about me if that happens?"

She glanced up at him and he saw that she had thought of it. She said firmly, "It isn't going to matter, Matt. They're planning murder and you're stopping them. It's the only thing you can do and I'm not going to blame you for doing it."

"And you'll wait for me here? You won't change your mind again and run away from me?"

She managed a small smile. "Not again, Matt. Not ever again."

He bent his head and kissed her on the mouth. Then he pulled away. "I'm leaving Chuck Sorenson. He'll stay here in the house. We're not going to let Wes and Rudy get out of the canyon if we can help it, but if they should happen to get away, we'll follow them and catch them before they can get this far."

She nodded. Suddenly she reached up and pulled his head down to her. She kissed him lingeringly, the way she had that night on the mountainside. He grinned at her when she broke away. "Much more of that and I won't even go."

She said shakily, "I'll walk out with you."

Halfway across the yard they met Chuck Sorenson; a stocky, bow-legged, middle-aged man heading toward the house.

Chuck was carrying a rifle and wore a revolver at his side. Matt said, "I don't think anything's going to happen, Chuck, but you keep awake. They'll try to get Chris and there's always the chance that something might go wrong."

"I'll watch, Matt. Don't worry."

Matt went on, with Josie walking beside him. One of the men brought him his horse but he didn't immediately mount. Looking up at the men he said, "If we don't have too much trouble crossing the river, we ought to get there well before the sky turns gray. We'll ride in, keeping as quiet as we can."

Josie said, "Matt."

"What?"

"They always have at least one man and sometimes two up on the hillside near the canyon mouth when they're expecting trouble. Maybe because of the rain they won't be there, but I wouldn't count on it."

"Can you tell me exactly where they'll be?"

"There's a sharp bend about a quarter mile from the canyon mouth."

"I know the place."

"It's straight up the hillside from that bend that they always wait. There are five or six big boulders up there and they've built a horseback trail to reach the place."

"We'll go up on foot. It's quieter."

He swung to the back of his horse. "Get back in the house as soon as we leave. Try and get Chris to go back to bed."

He turned his horse and rode out of the yard into the darkness. Looking back, he could see her standing there, tiny and defenseless but very straight. As he watched, she turned and walked toward the house and as she did, her shoulders slumped.

He felt a harshness in his throat. In spite of the brave front she'd shown him, she didn't expect him to return. Nothing had ever worked out for Josie and she didn't expect it to work out now.

Suddenly he was terribly angry with her wild, coarse family who never bothered to wonder what their women were feeling or what they wanted out of life. The Taskers were like animals, carnivorous animals who lived off their fellow men and who retired to their cave when pursuit came close and snarled at those thirsting for their blood outside.

Tomorrow, though, that was going to change. Outlaw Canyon would cease to be a refuge for killers and thieves. It would stop being a no-man's land because no one dared go inside. Fortress would be justified in whatever they did because they would have undisputed evidence against the canyon's inhabitants, evidence of rustling, still a hanging offense in this part of the land.

The trail dropped steeply away from the flat bench on which the ranch headquarters was built. The clay soil was slick as ice. The horses floundered and fought to keep their footing.

And the pines, the brush—everything Matt touched was dripping wet. In minutes he was soaked in spite of his heavy chaps.

He tried to calculate the time it would take them to reach the canyon mouth. He used to return from school in about two hours. But he had used the bridge crossing the river and the ground had not been slick.

Probably, tonight, it would take nearly three. If it took any more than that it would be light before they arrived. Even so, the sky would be getting gray in three hours more. They'd just have to make it in less.

Ahead of him, a horse floundered and went down with a crash, throwing his rider into the brush beside the trail. Matt halted his own horse and called, "You all right?"

A string of curses answered him. He yelled, "Get down off your horses and walk. At least until we get to the bottom of this hill."

He swung down himself and moved on ahead. He slipped and slid himself, but the high heels helped. Now all he had to do was keep out of his horse's way.

They were losing time by walking, but not very much. He didn't suppose any of the river bridges still held. They always went out in a flood as bad as this.

The minutes dragged away. He staggered against the rump of the horse ahead of him, recovered and seized the animal's tail. After that it was easier.

Soaked and bedraggled, they finally reached the bottom of the slope. And here they stopped, to check their gear, to curse mildly at their discomfort and to re-mount their horses before going on.

The river made a sustained and steady roar. Swimming horses across a torrent like that in the darkness wasn't going to be easy. Matt just hoped the crossing didn't consume more time than they could afford.

CHAPTER 15

Ten minutes later, Matt drew rein at the river bank. It seemed colder here than it had been in the trees and brush. The roar was louder too, and he could sometimes hear a log hitting a rock, or one scraping against the bank.

He glanced worriedly up at the sky. A few breaks were visible in the heavy cloud cover, and where these breaks occurred he could see the faint glow of the moon and stars beyond.

He stared out at the river again. It was like looking into a void, black and unbroken, and the only way he knew the river was there was by the sound.

He frowned. They had to cross, and they had to do it before daylight came. But maybe, if they rode downriver for a while before trying to cross, there was a faint possibility that the sky would clear. In moonlight, perhaps it wouldn't be so bad. There would be less chance of losing men.

He had to shout to be heard above the river's roar. "We'll ride downstream a ways. Maybe the sky will clear."

He could almost feel the relief in his men. Every one of them knew how deadly the river could be when it was flooding and filled with snags. If a man got separated from his horse he had no chance. He would drown and none of the others could help him no matter how they tried.

Matt reined his horse west and touched his sides lightly with the spurs. The horse broke into a floundering trot.

This way, the minutes dragged away. Matt reached the bridge he had used coming from school so many years before and stopped briefly. Nothing was left but the log abutments upon which the bridge had rested. The rest was gone.

He went on, using the road now that wound westward toward the town called The Forks, fifty miles away.

The moon broke through, illuminating briefly the angry floodwaters and then sailing behind a cloud again. Matt studied the sky. The clouds seemed thinner but whether they would break in time, he couldn't tell. In another thirty minutes they'd be opposite the mouth of Outlaw Canyon and they'd have to cross whether the clouds had broken up or not.

He found himself thinking of Chris, of the way the old man had aged in the last couple of years. He hoped that after tonight, Chris would be able to live out his remaining years in peace. If Wes wasn't killed, he'd go to prison for the theft of the Fortress cattle herd. And while that was going to hurt Chris, it wouldn't hurt him as much as having Wes trying to kill him so that he could inherit the ranch. Matt hoped Chris would never fully comprehend what Wes and the Taskers had planned for tomorrow.

The moon broke out of the clouds again. In its light, Matt saw the yawning mouth of Outlaw Canyon ahead and on his right. He glanced up. The clouds were moving rapidly but there was a large, clear space between the moon and the nearest clouds that could cover it.

He turned his horse through the thin fringe of brush between him and the river bank, his men following. He drew rein at the very bank and turned his head. "I'll go first. Come in behind me one at a time and about a hundred yards downstream from the man ahead of you. If one of you loses his horse, turn back toward the man behind. We'll have to make it fast because that moon isn't going to stay out long."

Nobody answered him. He waited a moment, then turned and put his horse into the river, which was shallow here next to the bank.

The animal fought for his head and tried to turn back, but Matt forced him to swim directly out and toward the other bank.

A floating tree loomed upstream from him, its branches reaching up from the torrent like clawing, twisted arms. A sinking feeling touched him. It seemed impossible that he could avoid the disaster and if he did not avoid it, both he and his horse would go rolling before the ponderous thing, to be swept under and kept there until they had drowned.

He reined his horse downstream and back toward the bank he had left only moments before. He held his breath briefly as the tree swept down on him.

He could see, now, what it was. A gigantic cottonwood, probably one undermined by past floods and leaning out over the river. This flood had completed the job begun by the previous ones. It had toppled the tree into the river and the current had torn it loose.

Its trunk, half submerged, looked as though it must be four or five feet through. And now, Matt noticed something he had not noticed before. The current was not deep enough here to float the tree and so it was rolling downstream like a gigantic tumbleweed. That rolling motion would catch a man and horse and drag them all the way to the bottom. Only when both were dead would it again raise them to the surface, perhaps to lift them high in the air on its entangling branches.

He shouted a warning to the men behind him on the bank, a warning not to enter the river until the tree had rolled past. But he knew his voice was lost in the roar and he could only hope no one had entered the river immediately behind.

Then the thing was on him, making a crackling, whistling sound, and a louder roar than that of the river itself because of the impediment it formed to the steady passage of current.

Matt tensed to leave his horse. A branch struck

him across the back, driving him against the withers of his horse and knocking the wind from him. The horse submerged, struggling violently.

Matt felt his own head go under, and held his breath. He clung desperately to the saddle horn, feeling the violence of motion, the tearing branches that seemed like live hands clutching at him.

This, then, was the end of everything. Tomorrow he and his horse would be left on some muddy bar by the receding waters, perhaps never to be found at all. The Taskers would succeed in their plan to seize Fortress and kill Chris. And Josie . . .

Matt's head broke water and he gulped air frantically. The sound was terrifying, but no longer, he realized, were those deadly branches striking him.

His horse's head broke water immediately afterward. Matt glanced around. The tree was past, rolling along with terrifying speed, diminishing in size rapidly with distance as it did.

The bank looked good to Matt and to the horse as well. The animal swam almost frantically, trying to reach it and the safety it represented.

Matt was so close he could see his men grouped there on the bank. He saw one enter the stream.

There was no time for rest, for recovery from terror, for anything now. He yanked his horse around, fighting his head upstream and then once more toward the far bank.

It didn't seem likely that anything like that

would come past again. He glanced up at the sky. The moon was very close now to the drifting clouds. There was barely time for him to get across before the river would be dark again.

He got the horse headed right and fought to keep him pointed that way. He dug spurs cruelly into the horse's sides.

The gigantic, rolling cottonwood was nearly out of sight downstream. Matt wondered if any of his men had been caught in it. He wouldn't know, he supposed, until he counted noses on the other bank, but he doubted if they had.

His horse began to tire, and swam sluggishly. Glancing around, Matt saw another man and horse only slightly behind him but quite a way downstream.

He slipped out of his saddle on the downstream side, retaining a grip on the saddle horn. The horse's body rose slightly in the water with his weight removed and the animal began to swim more strongly.

A floating, half submerged log struck the horse and drove a grunt from him, but it went on past without apparent injury to the horse.

Maybe, Matt thought, they should have entered the river farther upstream so that they could have swum with the current more, angling across slowly and thus avoiding most of this floating debris. But it was too late for such considerations now. They were committed, no matter how deadly this might be, no matter how heavy the cost.

He also knew that more than one man should have been left at Fortress or else Chris and Josie should have been sent to town, even at the risk of hurting Chris's pride. If Matt and his men didn't get across in great enough numbers to attack the canyon successfully, then Fortress and Chris were doomed.

Matt glanced around again, but he was now too low in the water to see anything. The first fringe of thin clouds was beginning to dim the face of the moon.

His horse turned downstream slightly and he couldn't stop him without mounting again. So he let him go. Looking ahead, he could see the yawning mouth of Outlaw Canyon sweeping swiftly past. He could also see the bank, less than a hundred yards away.

The horse apparently saw it too for he began to swim more frantically than before. At last the horse's feet touched bottom. An instant later, Matt touched bottom himself.

Current still tugged at them. But with purchase on the bottom, the horse lunged in great leaps toward the safety of the bank.

Thoroughly chilled and shivering, Matt let the horse drag him out of the water. He reached the bank and stood there a moment, head hanging, gasping for air. The horse stood listlessly, breathing hard.

Matt left him and returned to the river bank. He stared out across the torrent. The man who had been immediately behind him should be coming out now. He would be downstream by a couple of hundred yards.

The moon still shone dimly through the thin layer of clouds that had covered it. Matt glanced up and as he did it sailed into another clear patch of sky. With this added light, he searched the river again.

Downstream he saw a horse emerge from the water and an instant later saw a man swing up to mount. The man rode upstream toward him.

In the near darkness, Matt couldn't recognize him. He called, "Over here," and when the man reached him asked, "Were you second man in, or third?"

"Second. Right after you."

"Good thing you waited as long as you did. That cottonwood damn near got me."

"I saw it." The man shivered as though with a chill. "We thought it *had* got you, Matt."

Matt wished he had a smoke but he knew his tobacco was soaked. He asked, "Could you see the man behind you?"

"Sometimes. He ought to be coming out right now."

"Let's ride down that way. Maybe someone will need some help."

For the moment at least Matt had forgotten

Outlaw Canyon and the Taskers and the reason they were here. Foremost in his mind right now was the survival of his men. He mounted his horse and headed downstream, the other man following close behind.

The roar of the river made conversation impossible. Matt felt automatically for his gun and, reassured, went on.

They rode for about a quarter mile and picked up another man while they were doing so. Matt saw the second tree at about the same time the others did.

It was rolling along exactly as the first had done, but it wasn't quite as large. And then, almost immediately ahead of it, Matt saw a swimming horse and man.

He yelled, but he knew it did no good. He shouted, "Ride on downstream and gather the others up. We'll meet right here."

Even as he shouted, he spurred his reluctant horse back into the current. He felt the icy water close over his legs and slipped from the saddle as it did.

But he couldn't guide the horse or keep him from turning back, so he crawled back into the saddle again. Apparently the man toward whom he headed had not seen the tree. He was letting his horse tow him along and was on the downstream side of his horse.

Matt shouted at him again, but the roar of the river effectively drowned his voice.

The tree rolled ponderously along. Matt knew if the man had heard him when he shouted from the bank there would have been time for him to turn aside. But he couldn't have heard and Matt couldn't have made him hear. Not even if he'd emptied his gun into the dripping air.

He was now approaching the path of the ponderously rolling cottonwood. He was approaching the point of no return. If he continued, he would be swallowed up himself.

He'd never be able to reach the swimming man and horse even if he did. He yanked his gun from its holster and fired three times into the air. He saw the man raise himself out of the water, pulling himself up with the aid of the saddle horn. He saw the man's face turn toward the tree, almost upon him now.

Helpless, Matt watched as the man frantically climbed into the saddle and turned his horse downstream. For an instant it seemed as though he might make it and get away.

Then Matt saw one branch, longer and thicker than the rest, raise itself streaming out of the water on the upstream side of the tree. It made a slow, ponderous, threatening arc in the air as the tree rolled on.

Matt had to turn his horse to avoid the roots of the tree. He glanced back over his shoulder, watching as that reaching branch came down.

Faintly, even over the roar, he heard the man's

shout of terror as the branch came down on him. And then, so suddenly that it was frightening, the surface of the river was empty again. Empty except for that ponderously rolling tree.

There was nothing Matt could do. But he stayed in the river until he saw that particular branch roll out again on the upstream side of the tree.

Something was in it, smaller than a horse. It was the body of a man, caught in a crotch, wholly limp, wholly without movement of any kind except for that given it by the motion of the branch itself.

A shudder shook Matt and he turned his head away. Whoever that was, he was already dead. Even if it was possible to get him out of there, which it was not, it was too late now.

Where the horse had gone, Matt didn't know. He fixed his attention on the river bank and concentrated on getting there.

CHAPTER 16

Dripping and chilled, Matt rode out of the river and approached the silent group waiting for him at the appointed place. He knew they had seen the tree, knew they had seen the man and horse disappear before it. He asked, "Who was it? Who's missing?"

"It was Tate Johnson, Matt."

"Everybody else here?"

The men looked around, muttering almost as though to themselves. Matt counted. They were only missing one. All the rest had made it safely across. He glanced up at the sky. The moon had disappeared behind the clouds and the sky was wholly dark. No streaks of gray lightened the eastern horizon—yet.

Matt was shivering and he couldn't seem to stop. He knew they ought to have a fire, knew there really wasn't time. And yet, they had to have some light to check their guns and ammunition. They'd probably fight better if they weren't quite so miserable.

He said, "Come on. We'll build a fire near the mouth of the canyon and dry out some. That is, if there's any dry matches in this bunch."

Benny said, "I've got some, Matt. I always carry some wrapped in oilcloth in my saddlebags."

"Come on, then."

He led out upcountry toward the canyon mouth, holding his horse to a hard, fast, bone-jolting trot. He passed the canyon mouth and swung down beyond beneath a towering face of solid rock. He walked to the rock face and along it until he found a fissure that would hold a fire. He said, "See if there's any dry wood around."

Benny said, "I've got a little dry wood too. I always carry it in my saddlebags, wrapped in an old slicker. Not much but enough to start a fire with."

Matt grinned. "I suppose you've got coffee too."

"As a matter of fact I have. And a pot, and a couple of old tin cups."

Matt said, "Remind me to tell Chris you deserve a raise."

Benny didn't answer. He went to his horse, rummaged in the saddlebags, returned and knelt by the fissure in the rock. He began to make shavings with his pocket knife and a moment later a small flame began to grow.

Matt and the others searched close to the rock face for wood and found some that was not soaked through. They brought it and piled it beside the growing blaze. Someone took the coffee pot and went to the river to fill it.

The rock reflected the fire's light. The men gathered silently in a line facing it, turning occasionally to warm their backs. Their clothes began to steam. The aroma of coffee filled the air.

Matt glanced occasionally at the eastern sky. When everyone had sipped a little coffee from one of the two cups, he said, "All right. Check your guns and shells. Kill the fire and let's get out of here." No one had mentioned Tate and he knew that no one would. But he also knew all of the men were thinking of him, and remembering him, and seeing again the way he had died.

As they mounted up, Matt said, "Larry, you and Sam will come with me when we reach the place where their lookouts are supposed to be. We'll climb up, spreading out as we do. The main thing is not to make a damn bit of noise because we don't want a lot of shooting if we can avoid it. And don't be soft. These are rustlers and killers that we're dealing with."

"Don't worry about that, Matt."

"All right then. Let's go."

The column filed away, leaving a smoking, hissing pile of charred sticks against the rock.

At the canyon mouth, Matt slowed to a walk. The horses' hoofs made, at times, soft sucking sounds in the mud and there was the inevitable squeak of stirrup leathers, the occasional soft clang of metal against metal. All in all, however, their passage along the road was a quiet one.

Matt began watching for the spot Josie had described to him. It was difficult in the dark, but as they rode along the clouds thinned enough so that the moon, faintly visible through them, cast a small amount of soft light upon the land.

He had about decided that they had missed the place, and passed it, when he reached the sharp bend in the road he was looking for.

He halted and swung from his horse. He handed his reins to the man nearest him.

The creek, which tumbled along between the slope they must climb and the road, made a roaring sound not as loud as that of the river but loud enough, he hoped, to cover the unavoidable noises they would make climbing the dark, rocky slope.

Larry Jessup and Sam Gates took places on either side of him and together they waded across the creek, scrambling for footing on its rocky bed. Reaching the far side without mishap, they spread out and began to climb.

It was slow going and, Matt discovered, it was almost impossible to do it silently. His feet, in spite of the care he took, kept dislodging rocks. The moon darkened, then lightened again in time for him to see the huge boulders Josie had described ahead of him.

He glanced right and left, trying to see one of the others and failing to do so. He hoped they had all climbed at approximately the same rate of speed because they had to be together when they jumped the lookouts.

Ahead of him he suddenly heard a voice. "Hey Frank. Did you hear something?"

"Uh-uh. You're hearin' things."

"The hell I am."

"What do you think you heard, for Christ's sake?"

"I don't know. That damned creek is making so much noise down there. . . ."

Matt froze. He realized he was less than a dozen yards from the two men. He glanced to right and left but it was still too dark to see anything. There was a faint outline of gray silhouetting the ridge to the east of him, however, that he knew was beginning of dawn.

Time was rapidly running out. He took another careful step forward and yet another one. He felt with his foot each time he did.

Suddenly, to his left, he heard a rock grate against another rock, and afterward heard it roll noisily down the slope. The man ahead of him said sharply, "Hear that? Now by God do you believe I know what I'm talking about?"

There was no answer from the second man. Matt heard one of them moving cautiously toward the source of the sound.

In another few seconds there was going to be a flurry of gunshots up here, sounds that would carry to the Tasker place and bring the whole outfit out at a run. Unless Matt did something and did it fast.

Still trying to be careful of noise, but hurrying too, he swung and headed toward the place where he had heard the rock.

His eyes picked out the vague, blurry shape of a man ahead. He didn't dare call out and identify himself because if he did he would locate himself for the men above. He knew if he didn't call out he might be shot by one of his own two men.

The figure swung toward him just as another figure, approaching from above, merged with it.

There was a brief scuffle with its accompanying sounds. Matt plunged ahead, not caring now how much noise he made as long as he reached the struggling pair in time to take a hand and save his own man from injury.

He reached them and grunted softly, "Sam? Larry? Which one is you?"

One of the struggling figures answered him. Matt's gun was already fisted in his hand and he brought it swinging sideways against the head of the other man. Limp, the man slipped to the ground.

Sam was breathing harshly with exertion. He whispered softly, "Thanks Matt."

Matt didn't bother to acknowledge the thanks. He whispered, "Stay here. I'll circle and get behind the other one when he comes after you. He sure as hell heard all that noise."

"All right."

"And shoot if you have to. Don't worry about noise so much it gets you killed."

Sam didn't reply to this. Matt wondered where Larry was. Over on the right, he supposed.

He left Sam standing there, still breathing hard, and climbed carefully, angling to the left. He had gone no more than half a dozen yards before he stopped and waited, holding his breath and straining his ears.

From off on his right he heard a soft call, "Stacy? Where the hell are you? Is that you making all that racket down there?"

Matt's mind raced. If Frank received no answer he would know for certain that something had happened to his friend. He'd be doubly on guard, doubly nervous, much more likely to shoot at anything that moved.

Without thinking further about it, he grunted loudly and began to move noisily toward the voice of the other man.

He was committed now. But he figured, this way, that he could reach the man before the fellow realized that he wasn't Stacy. He could get close, maybe close enough to overcome him before Frank realized who he was.

He reached the trail that had been built to get horsemen up to this rocky, inaccessible place. On his right, now, he saw the dark figures of two horses and beside them that of a man.

Frank said, "Didn't find anything, did you?"

Matt grunted again and moved toward him, trying to appear unconcerned and indolent.

Twenty feet now separated him from Frank. Only twenty feet.

Suddenly, immediately below him on the slope, Larry lost his footing and fell. His gun clanged against a rock, making an unmistakable, metallic sound. And Larry himself uttered a low-voiced, involuntary curse.

Immediately the figure ahead of Matt tensed. Matt lunged toward him. He knew, immediately he did, that it was a mistake. He should have turned toward the sound as Stacy would have done. The fact that he did not tipped Frank off that he was a stranger, and dangerous.

Frank's gun bellowed almost in his face. He heard the angry buzz of the bullet, or perhaps he only felt its air. But it was an impression that he would not soon forget.

The flash nearly blinded him and then the echoes were rebounding from canyon wall to canyon wall, sounding like a fusillade of shots instead of only one.

He felt his hands touch Frank, then felt the rifle beneath his hands. He gripped it and wrenched viciously.

Frank held on, and was swung wildly across the narrow trail. His momentum at the end of the swing dumped Matt to the rocky ground, but he didn't let go of the gun.

Virtually blind in the almost complete darkness, they struggled silently and savagely for possession of the gun, for any advantage at all.

Matt turned the rifle loose. Frank fell back and

away from him. Matt snatched his revolver from its holster and plunged toward him. He met the rifle as Frank swung it, met it head-on in mid-swing.

It struck his shoulder, slid off and spent the rest of its force on the right side of his neck. Pain exploded from the area, but he was still in motion and the impact of the rifle couldn't stop him now.

His hand came down with a chopping motion and the barrel of his revolver raked Frank's head. The man fell back, with Matt clawing ahead to keep up with him. The revolver swung again.

This time it struck Frank's head squarely, with a dull, sodden sound. Frank went completely limp.

Matt didn't care whether he was dead or not. He didn't stop to look. Standing up he called, "Larry! Sam! It's all right and I'm coming down!"

He picked his way carefully down the rocky slope. The line of gray silhouetting the ridges to the east was plainer now.

Sam and Larry joined him and the three made their way to the gorge below. They mounted silently and, trotting their horses now, continued with the others up the canyon road.

CHAPTER 17

They had gone less than a mile, still riding as quietly as possible, when Matt's ears picked up the hoofbeats of a horse approaching them, fast, along the road. He said, "Get off the road. I'll tell him to stop. If he puts up a fight, cut him down but be careful where you aim. We don't want to be shooting our own men."

He didn't think the noise would particularly matter now. Wes, Olguin and the Taskers would know soon enough that they were being attacked.

The men broke ranks and left the road for the concealment of rocks and brush that bordered it. The pound of hoofs grew louder and a few moments later a rider thundered out of the gloom.

Matt bawled, "Hold it! Haul up and throw down your gun or you're dead!"

The man yanked his horse to a plunging, jumping halt, but he did not throw down his gun. He yanked it out and fired twice in the direction from which Matt's voice had come.

Matt stepped from behind the rock and fired as he did. The man jerked with the bullet's impact, then fell sideways and slid out of his saddle. He hit the ground with a thump and lay still, awkwardly sprawled in the mud. The horse, loose now, trotted away in the direction of the canyon mouth.

Matt swung to his horse and climbed the animal back on the road. He yelled, "Come on! It'll be light enough by the time we get in there."

The Taskers were undoubtedly up. They were probably just finishing breakfast, or just leaving the house preparatory to pushing the Fortress herd on out of the canyon mouth. Probably the cattle were corralled, or else they had been held in some small box canyon or pasture near the house.

Matt didn't know the inside of Outlaw Canyon at all. He'd never been this far before.

But it was getting lighter now. The whole sky was gray, and it was now possible to see for almost a quarter of a mile.

They traveled at a steady lope for another ten minutes and then, suddenly, broke out of the canyon and into a wide valley.

The house and outbuildings sat in almost the exact center of it. There were a couple of haystacks half a mile beyond the house. The cattle, close-herded, were moving toward the entrance to the gorge, and were about a half mile away.

Matt hauled up, searching for cover from which to fight. There was none. He turned his head and yelled, "Larry. Sam. Luke. Phil. You four come with me. The rest of you spread out and find cover on both sides of the entrance to the canyon. Don't let anybody through. Anybody, understand?"

The four separated themselves from the others.

Those who remained scattered to right and left, leaving their horses and climbing the hillsides, their rifles in their hands.

Matt stared ahead at the open valley. Those driving the cattle had stopped, apparently uncertain as to what they should do. Several men were visible near the house.

He realized that if he was going to exploit his advantage of surprise he had to do it now. He spurred his horse and, revolver in hand, rode at a hard run directly toward the Tasker house.

The other four followed close behind. Matt frowned as the distance dwindled between them and the house. There had to be a diversion of some kind, and fire would be the best. He felt no compunction about burning the Taskers out. Hadn't they planned to burn Fortress first? But he had no dry matches and he had left Benny Franks back there . . .

A thin plume of smoke rose from the tin chimney in the rear of the house. A kitchen stove, he thought. That was what he needed.

Turning his head, he bawled, "Keep 'em busy in front of the house!" What he had in mind was not only insolent; it was dangerous. Nobody had ever dared invade Outlaw Canyon before, let alone try what Matt had in mind.

They were well within rifle range now and he could see puffs of powdersmoke coming from the front windows of the house. He could see bullets striking in the soft, wet ground, tearing gouges sometimes a couple of feet long and sending up sprays of wet earth. But so far none of his men had been hit.

Only a hundred and fifty yards remained and that dwindled rapidly to a hundred, to fifty.

Matt and his men were firing now, firing at the puffs of powdersmoke in the windows of the house. He heard glass tinkle as one of the bullets broke a pane. Immediately behind him a horse went down, somersaulting wildly and throwing his rider a full twenty feet.

Matt couldn't even turn his head to see who it had been because they were now at point-blank range and he was swerving recklessly to get around the house.

His men swerved off the other way and made a wide circle preparatory to returning. Matt doubted if anyone inside the house had been hit. Shooting from the back of a running horse is doubtful business at best.

Immediately beside the back door, he swung to the ground and hit it running hard. The horse, well trained, slid to a stop in the mud. Matt slipped, recovered and dashed the remaining few feet to the door. He slammed inside, crossed the room running. He seized the hot kitchen stove near the bottom where it wouldn't burn his hands and lifted, heaving violently.

It overturned with a thunderous crash. Lids and

top spilled out on the floor, followed by the red-hot coals and burning wood that had been inside. Without waiting to see it catch, he whirled and ran back outside again.

His horse edged away from him nervously but Matt managed to catch him and swing to his back. Spurring savagely, he raced around the rear of the house, made a complete circle and rejoined his men a hundred yards from the front of the house.

He yelled, "Once more! One more circle and that fire will have had time to catch!"

Without slackening pace, the four thundered back at the house, firing recklessly as they did. Again the puffs issued from the windows.

Matt passed the downed man and saw that it was Sam Gates. There was a large red stain on Sam's thigh, but he was conscious and had his gun in his hand.

Matt yelled, "Larry! Pick Sam up and get him the hell out of here!"

He swerved off to the right directly in front of the house, hoping desperately that they could make this one last circle without anybody else getting hit. Smoke was boiling from the kitchen door and rising above the roof. He judged the fire had a good enough start now so that the Taskers couldn't put it out. He raced away, with Luke and Phil tearing along behind, apparently unhit. Larry had Sam up on his horse with him and was trotting away too. Matt stopped, jerked his rifle from the boot and, sitting there, began to fire systematically at the house, keeping the occupants busy until Larry and Sam could get out of range.

When he saw that they were safe, he turned away and, at a gallop, rejoined his men.

A pillar of smoke was now rising a hundred feet above the house. As he watched, flame licked out the door and up the shingled wall.

Matt bawled, "It worked! Now let's get Sam back where the others are so I can fix his leg!"

It took but a few moments to reach the entrance to the gorge. In the sparse brush there, Matt dismounted and lifted Sam down from his horse. He laid him on the ground and cut his trouser leg open with his knife.

The wound was bleeding freely and badly torn, but the bullet had missed the bone. Matt took off his jacket and removed his shirt. He ripped it down the middle, then wrapped it around the wound. Benny handed him a flat whisky bottle and he poured the contents liberally over the bandaged wound.

Sam turned pale and passed out. Matt got his slicker-wrapped blanket roll from behind his saddle, hoping the slicker had kept the blankets fairly dry.

He unrolled them and found the blankets damp outside the roll but nearly dry inside. He spread them over Sam. "We'll leave him here. He won't need anything for a while and the whole thing ought to be over in an hour or so. If it isn't, one of you can take him to town."

He turned away, wishing he had a smoke. He stared back at the burning house.

The Taskers were, apparently, making no effort to put out the blaze. He could see them down at the corral, catching and saddling horses. One of them mounted and raced away to the cattle herd which was now at a halt, grazing.

He grinned triumphantly. Josie had enabled him to turn the tables on them all right. If she hadn't come to Fortress last night, the cattle would be entering the gorge right now and half an hour from now would be outside, scattering. The Taskers would be waiting up in the rocks, waiting for Matt and his men to come riding in. And the butchering would be ready to start.

He said, "We'd just as well take it easy while we can. The next move is up to them."

The Taskers were all mounted now. They gathered in the yard between Matt's men and the burning house, apparently for a hasty council of war.

Matt could imagine their state of mind and, in spite of his misery, damp and chilled by the morning air, he had to grin.

The sun poked above the rocky ridges at Matt's back, throwing sunlight upon the rims at the far end of the valley and touching the higher places in the valley itself. But Matt and his men remained in shadow.

The whole house was ablaze by now. Flames and smoke poured from all its windows. In one spot, the flames had eaten through the roof and from this place a pillar of smoke poured, a pillar a thousand feet high.

The group in front of the house surged into motion. They spread out in a line as they came, leaving forty or fifty feet between each man. Like a line of cavalry men they came on at a gallop, heading straight toward the entrance to the gorge.

Matt yelled, "Get set! Aim for their horses! I don't want anyone getting through."

He crouched down behind a clump of brush, checking his rifle's loads. He waited, thinking how different was this situation from the one the Taskers had planned. Fortress's men were to have been the ones riding in the open to attack and the Taskers the ones hidden in the rocks. It must be infuriating to them to find themselves in such a situation.

An all-out attack wasn't the answer for them, however. It could only result in heavy casualties and little gain. Unless their intent was for two or three of their number to get through the gorge and outside no matter how high the cost to those remaining here.

They were now no more than four hundred yards away and the distance was closing rapidly.

Matt raised his rifle, taking a bead on the chest of one of the galloping horses.

He yelled, "Hold your fire until they're close enough!" and waited until the line of horsemen was less than a hundred and fifty yards away. Then he bawled, "Let 'em have it! Get their horses first!"

A ragged volley answered him. He felt his own rifle recoil against his shoulder and saw the horse he was aiming at somersault violently, throwing his rider clear.

Other horses were falling too. Along the line, four of them went down. Two lay still. The remaining two kicked and thrashed, but did not get up.

Only four mounts were left. They continued to gallop toward the gorge for an instant after the volley. Then, as though at a command, they veered aside and circled back.

Matt yelled, "Hold it!" as he saw the four whose horses had been shot from under them get up and begin to run back toward the burning house. He wasn't here to slaughter them, particularly when they were helpless and on foot. He had a feeling this battle had been won. The house was destroyed, the Taskers caught with stolen cattle in their possession. Conviction in the courts would be a certainty.

Later, he might regret the cease-fire he had yelled. Right now it seemed the only decent thing to do.

CHAPTER 18

The four remaining mounted men halted just out of effective rifle range and waited for the four who were afoot. Then, with each horse carrying double, they retired toward the house. As they did so, the house collapsed with a thunderous crash and a monstrous shower of sparks.

To Matt, they looked beaten. But they showed no signs of wanting to surrender. They rode to the corral and caught fresh horses for themselves. One went into one of the outbuildings and, when he came out, mounted and rode toward the cattle herd. Two of the others followed him.

The remaining five again rode toward the entrance to the gorge but not directly as they had before. They rode to a spot on the north side of it and here halted their horses and dismounted.

Matt frowned puzzledly. Obviously the Taskers had a plan but he couldn't imagine what it was.

Those who had ridden toward the cattle herd joined the single man who had been left there previously. They talked for several minutes. Then they separated. They rode to the up-canyon side of the herd and began bunching it.

Matt scowled. It looked as though they intended driving the herd out through the gorge though he could not imagine what their purpose could be in doing so. It was too late to get rid of the evidence now. Too many men had seen it here.

The four worked steadily, their shrill cries echoing from the steep rims beyond. The herd bunched and began to move slowly toward the entrance to the gorge.

Now, two of the drovers separated themselves from the remaining two. A feeling of uneasiness began to grow in Matt as they galloped, one to the right and one to the left of the entrance to the gorge. They dismounted at the foot of the rocky slope and, carrying rifles, began to climb.

Matt stood up. From the looks of things, those two climbing men would soon be above Matt and his party, and able to fire directly down on them.

He yelled, "Larry! Phil! One of you climb up on each side. Get those two before they get into position to fire down at us, or at least pin them down!"

As he finished, he heard a deep boom, like thunder, out in the middle of the valley. It was followed, immediately and before the echoes could start rolling back and forth, by another like it. He glanced that way as the echoes began to roll ponderously back and forth.

Two clouds of smoke were rising just behind the bunched cattle herd.

Comprehension flooded him instantly and he understood the Taskers' plan. One of them had gone to a shed near the house for dynamite a little while ago. Carrying it, he and two others had gone out and helped get the cattle headed toward the canyon entrance. The two who had separated themselves and begun to climb the slopes had done so for the purpose of forcing Matt and his men out into the middle of the entrance to the gorge.

Now the cattle were rumbling into motion, terrified by the two dynamite explosions so close behind. They were, Matt judged, about half a mile away.

He swung his head. The two men climbing the rocks were now almost immediately above, but were still slightly out of effective rifle range.

His own men, Larry and Phil, had stopped and were staring out into the valley at the stampeding herd.

It was a good plan and it was going to work unless Matt moved fast. He yelled, "Split up, one bunch to either side of the gorge. Get up on the hillside and out of the way!"

The crew jumped to their feet and began to sprint toward the hillsides. Matt roared, "Take your horses!" and swung his head.

The cattle were rumbling down upon them with frightening speed. They had already halved the distance separating them from the entrance to the gorge. Matt started to follow his men, then on impulse swung his head again toward the group of men who had earlier taken up a position to the north side of the entrance to the gorge.

These men had left that position and were now thundering toward Matt and his fleeing crew, firing as they came. They were trying to force the Fortress men to take cover in the path of the stampeding herd.

"Keep going!" Matt bawled. "Don't stop just because they're shooting at you! They can't hit a damn thing from the back of a running horse!"

Suddenly, then, Matt remembered Sam Gates, lying helpless and unconscious directly in the path of the stampeding herd. As he did, his heart sank. A few moments ago, overwhelming victory had been in his grasp. Now, through masterful tactics, the Taskers had reversed things completely.

He could hear the rumbling of the approaching herd. He seized his horse's reins and dragged him toward the place he had left Sam. Reaching Sam, he slammed his rifle into the saddle scabbard, then stopped and gathered the man in his arms. Sam was big, but Matt seemed to have extra strength in this moment of urgency.

He boosted Sam's unconscious body onto the horse, slinging it belly down across the saddle, taking a moment to hook Sam's belt over the saddle horn.

Guns were firing someplace but Matt didn't stop to look. He leaped astride his horse, sitting just behind Sam's body awkwardly, and gouged the horse with his spurs.

The terrified animal leaped ahead and ran. The

first of the cattle thundered past Matt, just behind him and less than a dozen yards away.

He angled toward the gorge itself to avoid the others. One collided with his horse.

Then he was clear, and in the rocks at the side of the gorge. He yanked his rifle from the boot, dismounted and swung around.

In this instant, the gorge entrance was choked with running cattle. But, looming above them, were the five horsemen who had earlier stationed themselves north of the gorge and who had, by firing at them a few moments before, tried to force Matt's men to take cover on the canyon floor.

Riding with the herd, they were hemmed in and crowded by terrified cattle on all sides.

And Matt understood the rest of the Taskers' plan. Timed perfectly, it had gone off like expertly conceived military strategy. Matt steadied his rifle on the rock in front of him and took a bead on the chest of one of the horsemen escaping with the stampeding herd. He squeezed the trigger carefully.

He heard the peculiar, unmistakable sound of his bullet striking flesh, but for an instant couldn't tell whether he had hit his man or just the horse. Then he saw the man fold forward, clinging to his horse's neck. He rode this way for twenty or thirty seconds, then slid sideways out of the saddle to disappear beneath the cattle's hoofs.

Immediately Matt drew a bead on another of the

rapidly moving riders. He fired, and fired again without success. The man was hopelessly out of range. But someone got a second man. Matt saw his horse go down.

The thing Matt had dreaded had happened after all. Wes, and Olguin, and one of the Taskers had gotten away.

The last of the herd was streaming past. The entrance to the gorge was now choked with cattle. As narrow as it was, it would be blocked for a distance of a quarter-mile.

He could get through, of course. But not as fast as he had to get through if he were to reach Fortress before Olguin, Wes and the man with them did.

His men were coming out of the rocks, leading their horses. Matt beckoned them to hurry. When they reached him, he said, "One of you take Sam to town to the Doc. Luke, you and Phil come with me. Wes and Olguin and one of the Taskers got out with that herd. They'll be heading for Fortress and we've got to beat them there."

He stared out into the valley. The Taskers' house was now a pile of charred and smoldering embers. One of the outbuildings had caught from it and was blazing furiously. He said, "The rest of you stay here. Those that are left will probably give themselves up. If they do, take them to town and turn them over to the sheriff."

He glanced over the horses of his men, picked

the strongest looking one in the lot and swung to his back. He didn't want to move Sam again and Sam was lying across Matt's horse.

He rode toward the canyon mouth, with Luke and Phil immediately behind.

They were able to make good time for about a mile. Then they ran into the cattle, stopped now and solidly blocking the road.

They forced their way through slowly. Impatience that bordered on panic touched Matt. Wes and his two companions were far ahead, probably out of the canyon by now.

How could he have been caught like this? He blamed himself until he realized that, no matter what he'd done, he couldn't have kept the three from getting out. If he'd taken his crew out into the valley he'd have left the entrance unguarded and the trio would have gotten away anyhow.

He had, at least, upset the part of their plan that would have permitted them to escape responsibility for killing Chris. But that wasn't going to help if Chris was dead.

And Josie was in mortal danger too. When they found her at Fortress with Chris they would know she had warned Matt of their plan. They would realize they could not count on her silence. And they would probably kill her too.

Matt dug spurs into his horse's sides and the animal pushed forward against the cattle more vigorously than before. But it seemed to take forever, getting through. The cattle were jammed too tightly together.

Matt yelled, and slapped his chaps with the ends of the reins. When his horse would have stopped, Matt spurred him mercilessly and made him go on.

Ten minutes passed, fifteen. Matt could see, ahead now, the thinned-out edge of the herd.

He drew his gun and fired it several times into the air. The herd ahead of him began to move.

Then they were through the close-packed part of it and could lift their horses to a trot, counting on the cattle to make way for them. When he passed the last few animals, Matt spurred his horse to a steady lope.

Running the horse steadily wasn't going to help. Neither he nor the others could run all the way to Fortress.

They passed the body of the man Matt had killed coming in, lying in the road. His horse was standing a short distance beyond. Matt rode to him, caught him and quickly changed mounts. After that he increased his pace for he knew this horse was fresh. His men began to fall behind.

He turned his head and yelled, "Make it as fast as you can! I'm going on ahead."

They raised their hands to wave acknowledgement. Then Matt rode around a sharp bend in the road and lost sight of them.

A few minutes later, he rode out of the canyon.

He stared ahead anxiously, hoping to see the three who had gotten out ahead of him. But he saw nothing at all.

The river was down considerably from where it had been last night. Matt put his horse into it without leaving the saddle, keeping a wary eye upstream for floating debris. There was some, but it was mostly small stuff that he avoided with ease.

He climbed the horse out on the other side and forced him to a trot in spite of the grade they had to climb. The night and the morning following had been filled with death and destruction and it wasn't over yet. Balked and defeated, Olguin, Wes and whichever of the Taskers was with them would be much more dangerous now than they had ever been before.

CHAPTER 19

Matt had never been an impatient man. Yet never in his life had there been this urgency in getting where he had to be.

He tried to guess how far ahead of him the others were. If they had a fifteen minute start, which they undoubtedly did, they would reach Fortress with enough time to get the house afire and kill its occupants before he could arrive.

Nor were the odds very favorable. Matt was all alone, pitting himself against three. He could only hope that Chris and Josie and Chuck Sorenson could hold them off for a little while, that they would not be caught by surprise when the three arrived.

He knew each landmark along the way and he marked them off in his mind with agonizing slowness. He crowded the horse until the animal was lathered and wheezing, and only then did he stop long enough for it to catch its breath.

The sun rose in the cloudless sky and the land began to steam with its warmth. Looking back from a high promontory, Matt saw that the river valley was filled with fog.

But the ground was firmer today. His horse had no trouble with his footing except in a place or two.

A mile from the house, Matt could stand it no

longer and put the horse into a hard run, careless of brush that clawed at him, careless of an occasional bit of treacherous going underfoot. The horse faltered and stumbled, but recovered and went on. Matt had never in his life used a horse this way. The animal was ruined even if he didn't die.

Half a mile yet remained. He strained his ears, listening for sounds, for shots. But he heard nothing.

The horse fell while he was still several hundred yards short of the house. Matt left the saddle before the animal collapsed and hit the ground running.

His rifle was in his hand and, as he ran, he checked his revolver to be sure it was seated in its holster. Then he broke into the clearing that held the ranch buildings and the house and hauled up short.

Three horses were standing beside the barn, on the side away from the house. But he saw nothing else.

For several minutes he stood motionless, waiting until he would see something move, or hear some sound that would tell him where they were. They'd not hesitate an instant about cutting him down, from ambush or from behind. And while he wasn't afraid of them, he knew too much was at stake to rush into this unthinkingly.

When nothing had moved or made a sound for

the short time he stood waiting, he began to cross the yard, rifle at ready, half crouched and prepared to dive for shelter the instant there was need for it.

He reached the corner of the barn and from here he could see that the back door of the house was open. Then they were inside the house. Or some of them were. And he might already be too late.

He tensed, preparatory to making a run for the door, and as he did he heard the faintest of squeaks above him and to his left.

Instantly he dived ahead, around the corner of the barn.

A gun blasted behind him and the bullet kicked up a shower of damp earth six feet from the corner of the barn. Without hesitating, Matt broke into a run.

A window crashed as it was broken, an upstairs window in the house. A rifle roared up there and roared again.

Matt reached the barn doors, one of which was open by about a foot. He flung himself inside, falling as he did.

Instantly, from the loft, a revolver barked again. The bullet tore into the door, tearing a shower of splinters from it.

Matt crawled frantically for the shelter of a broken bale of straw. The revolver crashed again, but this time Matt couldn't tell where the bullet went.

He was behind the straw bale now. It wasn't

where he wanted to be, yet he knew that until he eliminated the man in the barn loft, he hadn't a chance of reaching the house. He supposed the man in the loft had been watching the house when he arrived, which would explain why he hadn't been seen. Or perhaps the man had expected him later, not realizing he had obtained a fresh horse.

Lying motionless behind the straw bale, he glanced upward toward the loft. There was an opening immediately in front of the door that was used for loading wagons with hay from the loft. He could see into the loft through it. There was no cover for a man up there and if whoever it was moved enough to see Matt and shoot him, he would be exposed himself.

Timbers and floorboards creaked slightly in the loft as the man moved. Matt got to his feet. He could follow the man by the sounds he made, an advantage the man in the loft didn't have. He could wait, and conceal himself, knowing exactly where his adversary was, until the man showed himself.

But there wasn't time for such a careful game of cat-and-mouse. Over at the house, Chris might already be dead. Josie might be hurt. . . .

Matt moved swiftly after that, along the alleyway, running down the center of the barn, his footsteps cushioned by the thick carpet of dry manure that covered the floor. He reached the ladder at the far end of the barn before the man above reached the center one.

He climbed it, remembering that it creaked, and poked his head and rifle barrel above the floor level of the loft simultaneously.

Olguin—it was Olguin—lay flat on the loft floor facing Matt. His head was poked down below the level of the floor as he searched for Matt beneath. At any instant Olguin would see the lower part of his body on the ladder at the end of the barn.

He yelled, "Olguin!"

Olguin yanked his head up, raising his revolver in the same movement. Matt brought his rifle to bear.

And suddenly he realized he had made a disastrous mistake. He had forgotten that he stood on the rungs of a ladder, that he needed to steady himself with one hand, that a rifle was virtually useless unless held steady by both hands. He felt himself falling and saw Olguin's revolver gaping him.

Matt fell back. He knew that the edge of the opening would stop him but he also knew that if he wasn't dead when it did, he would be badly off balance and perhaps in a position from which it would be extremely awkward to shoot.

He was faced with a choice, one that had to be made in the lightning part of a second. He could fall to the floor below and probably save his life. Or he could try scrambling part way out onto the loft floor into a position from which he could shoot at Olguin.

He slammed the rifle down onto the loft floor and leaped upward and out onto it.

Olguin's gun discharged. Had not Matt moved when he did, the bullet would have taken him straight through the chest where it had been aimed. As it was, it caught him in the ribs, tearing a furrow several inches long and deep enough to crack a rib. From a crouch, he snatched up his rifle and brought it to bear on Olguin.

He fired at almost the same instant that Olguin fired for the second time.

The realization that this man facing him was the one who had so brutally manhandled Josie was perhaps not a conscious one in his mind. There was no time for conscious thoughts. But it was there, in whatever form.

His bullet took Olguin in the arm, tearing through it just above the elbow and shattering the bone. Olguin's bullet, fired at almost the same instant Matt's struck, was deflected and went into the wall of the barn a foot away from Matt's head.

Matt jacked another cartridge into the rifle, following Olguin with the muzzle as he did. Shock was apparent in Olguin's face, as was the surprise that always comes to a fast gunman when he faces death. He was left only with his left arm, which Matt had previously broken and which had not healed completely straight.

But he seemed to know that mercy was something he could not expect from Matt. He dived to the floor for his fallen gun.

He reached it, clutched it with his left hand, rolling as he did. It poked awkwardly out from beneath his body but its muzzle was steady and swinging again toward Matt.

Matt fired a second time, this time less hastily.

This bullet took Olguin in the throat, a couple of inches higher than it had been aimed. Blood gushed from Olguin's severed jugular vein, drenching the floor on which he lay almost instantly. Spreading, the bullet shattered his spinal column as it emerged at the rear of his neck.

He made no movement after it struck, no voluntary movement at least. His body slumped against the floor, eyes glazing and empty. Reflex discharged the gun he held in his left hand, since only the tiniest amount of pressure on the trigger was required to fire it. But this bullet, too, was wild.

Matt stood up. He realized his hands were shaking violently. For several seconds blood pumped from the hole in Olguin's neck and this eerie evidence of life after death unnerved Matt. He turned his head away.

He took a few breaths to compose himself. Then, after jacking a fresh cartridge into the rifle and replacing those he had used from his pocket, he climbed shakily down the ladder to the floor of the barn beneath.

The most difficult part of the task still awaited him. Wes and one of the Taskers were over at the house.

If they had not already disposed of Chris, Josie and Chuck, there was everpresent danger that they would before Matt could interfere. In addition, getting to the house now was going to be almost impossible. A full hundred and fifty feet separated it from the barn, every foot of that distance open and bare as a tabletop.

Matt walked along the alleyway toward the big front doors. And as he did so, a horse in one of the stalls nickered with fright and pulled at his halter rope.

CHAPTER 20

He whirled around and stared at the horse. He stood motionless for several seconds, then turned and stared at the big double doors through which he had entered the barn.

After that, he walked along the alleyway, picking up a pitchfork as he went. He reached the doors and, standing as far back as he could, put the tines against the door.

Suddenly he lunged forward, forcing the fork against the unbarred door, slamming it violently open with the pressure he exerted on the fork. Before it completed its swing, he threw himself sideways, falling, rolling as soon as he struck the ground.

Sound erupted over at the house, the crashing sound of a revolver triggered as rapidly as possible. Three or four bullets came through the open door and tore into the manure-covered floor of the barn, kicking up small showers of the dusty stuff.

Grinning, Matt got to his feet. Avoiding exposure in the door opening, he retreated along the barn alleyway to the stall where the horse was tied.

He stood his rifle against the stall and took down a bridle hanging on a nail. He went into the stall and slipped it onto the terrified horse over the halter he already wore. Then he untied the halter rope and led the horse from the stall.

He didn't know if he was going to get away with this, but it was the best chance he'd thought of yet. He picked up his rifle again and vaulted to the bare back of the horse.

He waited, holding the terrified horse still with an inflexible hand on the reins. He didn't want to go out just yet. Those at the house were nervous and ready for him right now. Give them time to wonder; give them time to tire and look away. Give them time to puzzle over what he intended doing next.

Though waiting was hard, he forced himself to wait almost five minutes. Then, stiffening, he leaned forward and dug his spurs savagely into the horse's sides.

The animal leaped forward, startled, and thundered down the alleyway toward the open door. Matt lay close against his withers so as to clear the top of the door, also with the purpose of presenting as small a target as possible when he thundered into the open beyond the door.

The door started to swing shut, pushed by the wind outside, and for the briefest moment of panic, Matt wondered if he would get through it before it swung completely shut. If the horse piled up against the door and fell, he'd be finished. Afoot, in that open space between barn and house, he wouldn't have a chance.

He felt the door brush his leg as it closed against the running horse and then he was in the open, moving with terrific speed directly toward the house.

The gun in the upstairs window roared, again and again and again. But not a one of the bullets even came close to him. He had taken the man, whoever he was, completely by surprise.

The horse veered to avoid the house, and as he swerved, Matt left his back.

His body struck the wall of the house with a crash that shook it and knocked the rifle from his hands. Half stunned, he recovered and picked the rifle up. Then, without hesitation, he slammed into the kitchen.

He thought he understood why they had waited, why they had not already set the house ablaze. They knew he would come, knew he would not be far behind. And they wanted him, wanted him dead almost as much as they wanted Fortress Ranch.

The kitchen was empty, but he had expected that. There now remained for him only the task of getting upstairs.

Only that task, he thought wryly. Only the task of getting upstairs against the determined opposition of Wes and the Tasker brother who both wanted to kill him almost as much as they wanted to go on living themselves. He'd managed a ruse getting to the house but there was no ruse that would get him safely up the stairs.

He discarded the rifle and pulled his revolver from its holster at his side. He checked the loads in it and worked the action to be sure mud and water hadn't ruined it. Then he crossed the kitchen like a cat.

He kicked the door open and stood just short of the opening for an instant before he lunged on through.

There was a big, leather-covered chair just beyond the door and he threw himself toward it, crouching soon as he reached it.

But no shots racketed through the house. It was so silent it might have been empty of human life.

He got up and raced toward the stairs. Something caught his eye behind the sofa and he veered that way, gun ready in his hand.

He dropped down behind the sofa just as a gun blasted at the head of the stairs.

There was a body here, lying on its face. He didn't have to turn it over to know who it was. Chuck Sorenson.

Matt reached out and picked up his wrist. He felt for pulse but could detect none. He shifted his grasp and suddenly felt it, faint, but regular.

He turned Chuck over, careful not to expose himself to the marksman at the head of the stairs. There was a nasty gouge on the side of Chuck's head, reaching from the forehead all the way to the back of his head. It was bleeding slowly, but blood was already beginning to clot in it.

If he could only bring Chuck to, he thought. The

man couldn't fight in the condition he was in. But perhaps he could divert their attention long enough to be useful.

They undoubtedly thought Chuck was dead. He must have fallen as though he was when he got that crease.

Water. If he only had some water. But he hadn't and he didn't dare leave here now.

He frowned. Then the frown disappeared. He dug a hand into his hip pocket and brought it out clutching a bandanna. The bandanna was damp from the soaking it had gotten when he swam his horse across the river.

He spread it out and folded it twice. Then he laid it on Chuck's forehead and pressed it down.

Chuck started to groan, but Matt clamped a hand over his mouth. Chuck's eyes came open.

Matt waited until the blankness left them, until he saw recognition in them. Then he whispered slowly, "Chuck. Can you hear me?"

Chuck nodded weakly.

"Think you can get up?"

Chuck nodded again and stirred.

"I want you to get down at the other end of this sofa and throw three or four bullets at the head of the stairs. They think you're dead and they'll think it's me. When they expose themselves to shoot back, maybe I can get a shot in myself."

Chuck nodded. Matt took his hand away from the man's mouth and Chuck rolled and pushed himself to his hands and knees. His gun was lying on the floor. Matt picked it up and replaced the empty loads. He handed the gun to Chuck.

The man crawled carefully to the other end of the sofa. Matt stationed himself at the opposite end, gun in hand, waiting.

Chuck stuck his head out and rapidly fired three shots toward the head of the stairs. Sound filled the room and acrid-smelling powdersmoke clouded the air.

Instantly, almost, Chuck's gun was answered by the one above. Chuck ducked back and Matt threw himself recklessly into the open.

He saw Wiley Tasker at the top of the stairs, crouched, resting his weight on one hand while the other held a smoking gun. Matt raised his gun as Wiley's began to swing toward him. Wiley's eyes were wide with startled surprise because Matt, whom he had believed to be at the other end of the sofa, had somehow gotten to this end with astonishing speed.

Matt felt his gun recoil against his hand. The bullet hit the top step, showering Wiley with splinters. Matt fired again.

Wiley started to straighten up. Then he folded forward and came rolling down the stairs.

Matt yelled, "Watch him, Chuck!" and leaped to his feet. Running, he cleared Wiley's rolling body as it hit the bottom of the stairs and went on up, taking the stairs three at a time.

He was gambling everything on the hope that Wes was with Chris and Josie, that Wiley had been the one who had been watching for Matt. He doubted if they would leave Josie and Chris alone, doubted if they'd have taken that chance.

He made it to the top of the stairs. Seeing nothing there, he halted, trying to guess which room they were in. He didn't dare guess wrong. As soon as Wes realized that both Wiley and Olguin were gone he probably would kill both Chris and Josie in sheer desperation.

And then he heard a scream—from Chris's room, he thought. He whirled and raced that way.

He slammed into Chris's room so hard that he nearly tore the door from its hinges. It crashed back against the wall, then rebounded, striking him as he came through.

And as he charged, he understood Josie's scream. Chris sat on the bed and Josie stood pressed against the wall in back of him. Wes sat in a chair, the gun in his hand leveled at Chris's chest.

Wes had been deliberately taking aim on Chris, he realized, and that had brought from Josie an involuntary scream. But now Wes tried to turn, tried to bring the gun to bear on Matt.

No time now for sparing Chris. At point-blank range, Matt fired.

The bullet smashed solidly into Wes's chest, its impact great enough to drive him sideways, toppling the chair, dumping him to the floor with a thunderous crash. Matt fired again as he hit the floor.

Wes didn't move after that. Matt stared down at him in surprise. It was over. It was all over now. It had been far too close but it had come out all right.

He felt weak with relief. He realized that his whole side was soaked with blood and he felt pain, sharp and burning, for the first time in the wound along his ribs.

Josie put her hands over her face. She began to shake violently. Chris stared up at Matt from the bed, as though dazed.

Matt turned and walked to the door. He yelled, "Chuck?"

"It's all right, Matt. Wiley's dead."

Matt turned and went back to Chris. He said, "Let's go downstairs and get a drink. I think you could use one and I know damned well I could."

Chris got up. He glanced at Wes, lying on the floor. Then he walked to the door strongly, as though a great weight had been lifted from him.

Matt went to Josie. She took her hands away from her face and looked at him. Her heart was in her eyes and her mouth was trembling and he knew that, as long as he lived, that look would never fade from his memory. He said, "Come on downstairs. Come on. It's time to start living again."

She fled to his arms and he held her tightly

against him for a long, long time until her trembling body stilled, until calm came to her twisted face and tortured eyes.

He didn't see Wiley's body when he got downstairs and supposed Chuck had either dragged it outside or behind the sofa where it wouldn't show. Chris had a bottle and glasses on the table and was pouring each one half full.

He looked at Matt and at Josie and he managed to smile. He said, "We all need this drink and I know it's no time for a toast but I'm going to make one anyhow. Let's drink to the kids that are going to fill this house. Let's drink to the grandchildren I'm finally going to get."

Matt looked down at Josie and she gazed back at him steadily. He said, "We'll work at it, Chris." The three of them drank and then they all walked out together into the sunlight.

Center Point Publishing

600 Brooks Road ● PO Box 1
Thorndike ME 04986-0001 USA

(207) 568-3717

US & Canada:
1 800 929-9108
www.centerpointlargeprint.com